The Other Side

The Other Side

Stories

E. Thomas Finan

THE FIELDNOR PRESS
BOSTON

The Other Side

Copyright © 2010 by E. Thomas Finan

www.fieldnorpress.com

ISBN 978-0-9828497-0-5

To my parents

Contents

Lucy *di Sartoria*

10:55

"There—there—turn your chin just a little more to the left. Little more. Little more. Ah-ah-ah there. Hold it. That's a good angle." She didn't know if her husband was praising her for embodying that angle or himself for noticing its goodness. Considering the way his lips curled as he swirled his brush in the paint globbed on his palette, she figured it was the latter. He had assumed his standard costume for painting: the blue-and-black plaid shirt and dark stained jeans. The black-rimmed glasses, too, were now part of his painterly iconography. The strands of his dyed brown hair reached over the top of his balding head like gnarled, withered fingers. The legs of the steel chair were cool against her bare ankles. He had wanted her that way, with her knees slightly splayed out, so that was how she sat. Part of the chair's back drove against her spine. She shifted a little.

Drew almost looked petulant. "Lucy?" Her name was like a rebuke, like a toddler's whine. But Drew's self-pity twisted into self-congratulation. "This should be a good pose. Very nice. Very nice. Good for the lines." The "lines" would be running diagonally across the massive (and presently blank) five-by-eight-foot canvas leaning against the wall. An image of her would be on that canvas, somewhere. Drew was very pleased with the size of the canvas, the difficulty of navigating it up the stairs to his loft studio, the ladder he was going to need to paint on it. This session was for a study. "I mean it," he had once said, "to mix graffiti and studio standards, mechanic lines and the organic human form, to destabilize the often implicit relations of pop art and the classical." He sometimes fantasized about the reaction to *work #9*—if it would get any headlines, maybe help with a few grants or some better commissions.

But today he was not bruiting to himself or her about the possibility of acclaim. Instead, as he dashed his brush across the smaller canvas in front of him, he complained. He had been looking forward to the *Edge Review* profile for weeks. Only, when the magazine arrived in its plastic wrap, he found out that this profile was not exclusively about him. It surveyed the contemporary Brooklyn art scene. Oh, he was prominently featured—he got a whole section to himself—but it was still an unpleasant surprise. And the actual comments! Not only was he pushed to a secondary spotlight; its glow was not always golden yellow. "I mean that's crap—complete and utter crap—about that 'slight softening with middle age of his keen eye and brush.' They spend—what?—*two* paragraphs on my Waterfront and *Duex Heures* shows! Do you even know how many critics (and I mean real critics, not these Abe Fox wannabes) have come up to me and told me that those were some of the best and most influential exhibitions of the '80s? Does this *Tania Hocks* know?" His speech was a bobbing chain of mutters. At moments, it reached a strangled crescendo. "That's right: give the old man a few pats on the head and usher him away to make room for these newer talents. Well, I'm not so old. And I'm not done yet. And I'm not going to stand aside for some *pisher* like HK Beryl."

    11:23

She remembered once, at an art opening, how triumphant Drew had seemed. He always loved to take her to those openings, always loved to say—just a little too loud—through the milling crowd that reminded her of a bunch of uncomfortable skeletons, "Yes, that's my *wife*." Sometimes, he would stand and just watch her talk and see the eyes of other men fix on her with desire even as his own gleamed with inflated pleasure. Sometimes, his eyes seemed like they were watching a pornographic movie as they took in the spectacle. One night, he had been flush not only with the wine and, in a corner, he had drawn her close to him and said softly in her ear, his breath heavy and sweet, "It's wonderful to be admired." His throat had squeezed those syllables the way he clutched her body when they had sex.

11:32

"It's dreck piled on dreck. That's what it is. They're just ravens. Ravens and crows. But, still, that was a nice phrase: 'the effortless grace of his challenge to reigning hegemonies.' A really nice phrase. And that was a nice picture of me. Gotta give the photog credit."

She had seen that gripping desire from the first moment in his eyes. They had met at an opening for one of his friend's photography series. She was the chief model, and all the photos were nudes. So they had met flanked by two five-by-eight blow-ups of her naked, black-and-white body. Her flesh, which the photographer had misted with water every few shots, had seemed like gleaming metal. She had known the desiring looks of men in multitudes before—dancing in music videos, walking the runway—but his eyes seemed to scoop her away from that crypt; they reached forward and held her tight, tight as his hand on hers when they were introduced. "A fine subject," he had said.

11:51

"But it just comes back to what I always say: you can't account for bad taste. And they're always looking for something new. Well this'll give them something new."

She shifted in the chair again. The steel was poking. She was hungry. She could only take so much more of the spectacle of her husband whining.

He noticed her movement. "Just a little more."

11:54

Another shift. She squirmed. He squiggled a little more with his paintbrush, though now it seemed more an attempt to annoy her, to draw out her waiting, than anything else. However much he had seemed to flicker in life, Drew always did have vast reserves of peevishness. No, that peevishness was flickering, too; he couldn't even commit to annoying her. "Well, that's—that's good." He smiled, unctuous, wheedling.

12:07

After changing her clothes, she slipped her pocketbook over her shoulder and crossed to the front door. It was so hot that afternoon, within those walls. Standing in the hallway, his face pinched again over the *Edge*, Drew raised his head.

"I'm going out."

"Out?"

"Out," she said, and slammed the door behind her to shut out any more pestering words.

They both knew where she was going. She could hear beneath that patina of sharpness in his question a plaintiveness, as though that edge were a way of keeping a grip on his own feelings. They both knew. That knowledge was like a bee buzzing between her collar and her neck.

Looking for a spot for a gallery had been another patina, another dusty facade. It didn't have to take over a year to look for a location, but it did with Cal as her agent. Drew never asked why exactly it took so long; he didn't need to—didn't dare to. It would be an investment, he had said.

The buzzing intensified. Maybe it was that buzzing that hollowed out the clicks of her heels on the pavement today. They rang thin and attenuated through the din. She walked a block, and they grew thinner still—tiny, like pins. What was that figure stalking her? Was it there, close as her shadow, ready to tap her on the shoulder in an instant? She kept walking. Faster, faster. Tiny tiny *click*s, like a crab scuttling on a cookie sheet.

She walked down a few blocks, took a few turns. There it was: the gleaming red '65 Corvette. That was one of Cal's favorite toys. There he was, waiting outside the car. Sunglasses. Chinos. Black blazer. Pink shirt, the tips of its open collar spread out like greedy hands. "You're looking cheery today," he said.

"Thanks."

As he held open the car door, he was smiling that usual little ironic smile, the one wry to the fact that he couldn't—that she wouldn't let him—kiss her in public. But he could hold open a car door for her, with that bow mocking chivalry.

"I see hubby's good mood is rubbing off on you." He never had any problem mentioning her husband, even if she did these days. It was like it didn't really matter to him—just another topic for his amusement. And, by the time he was at the wheel, he had switched to another diversion. "So—lunch?"

She nodded.

He smiled and put his foot to the gas.

They crossed through the narrower streets of Brooklyn, over the bridge, to the tall spires of Manhattan. Cal loved Manhattan—or at least didn't roll his eyes at it the way he did at Brooklyn. "It's for the ants," he would say, and Cal Trifft was not an ant.

As they drove over the water, Lucy remembered the early thrill of riding with him in the Corvette, with the wind rushing through her hair. The hum of the motor had seemed to reach right up through her waist to her breasts—a fluttering in her ribs. She had wanted to laugh, then, along with the racing wind and the sky-scrapers glittering with the sun.

She had met Cal about a year ago. He was into real estate. It was at some awards ceremony, something about civic recognition. His girlfriend at the time had gone, pulling him with her. Lucy had noticed him hanging around the bar, his blondish hair amiably mussed, his lips set—she couldn't tell at the time—in a curl of amusement or boredom. Drew had been worm-ing his way into some board members' circle, and she had crossed the ballroom to the bar. With a word of small talk from her, his eyes focused in an instant, and the curve of his smile reminded her of the edge of a falcon's beak. It scooped her away from that sterile hubbub. She mentioned the gallery idea. A few days later, after going over some possible locations, they shared their first kiss.

There had been that thrill. The thought of that batted at her through the maelstrom of lunch. It was the usual topics: business, the personal lives of the city's elite, examples of vice and the ridiculous. Cal sneered and poked through much of the meal. Lucy chewed on her salad in silence. "And I told him you're not gonna get a rate like that: Manhattan ain't Detroit.

What's he gonna try to find next—an old Ford factory? But he just kept nodding his dumb trust-fund-baby head, saying that he'd keep looking. Well, five weeks later he comes back. Yeah, he's looked." Guffaws over the prime rib. "So much for that dream." More laughter.

After stuffing the black bill folder with twenties and handing it to the waiter, Cal reached under the table. His hand groped for her thigh. He smiled, and his eyes seemed like pieces of blue steel. Before, those fingers tightening might have sent her flesh all quivery. Here was a man. Strong and certain, like a hawk swooping through the fog.

Why did the restaurant—big, crowded, bustling with money—seem cold and blank, like she was alone in a doctor's office?

"Well?" he asked with a cocked eyebrow.

She didn't say anything at first; her hands stayed folded on her lap. Cal would have sex anytime and anywhere. He liked variety. Sometimes, it would be his penthouse. Other times, some five-star hotel suite or a little motel in Jersey. Once, she had flown—for a fashion show, she told Drew—to Florida. Cal had had business there, too. Champagne every night. The silk sheets the faintest breeze of the sea would send rippling. The sunlight languorous and thick. The shuffling waves of the sea, like a man humming in her ear. The sand, soft and smooth, that soaked up the sun's heat and stuck to her skin.

Before, there might have been some flush within.

"Alright," she said.

Later, the sun had begun to set. She could see traces of orange through the hotel's cheap, thin curtains. The sheets smelled of sex and just a little sweat. Turning her face in the pillow, she could smell a hint of his cologne, or maybe his shampoo, through the bland odor of the cleaning service's detergent. Cal didn't care for cuddling. He was in the bathroom, taking a shower. She heard his steps through the hiss and fuzz of the water. It seemed like an old TV show, happening a thousand miles away.

It had been whatever it was. Quick, slow, it didn't matter. It left her empty, heavy with emptiness. With her ear to the pillow she could hear her pulse, thick and slow, like her heart was twitching through molasses.

The emptiness, that confusion, had slowly crept up on her. She tried to wait it out, but still it rose. She smoothed her hair, but her hand soon caught in her highlighted tangles. She could feel that thick pumping even in her brain. Through the molasses, a few turning questions. Why had there been, perhaps, some sigh of relief as Cal's limbs unwound from hers? Why was there this emptiness?

Cal walked through the door. Other than the towel around his neck, he was naked. She knew that he was vain about his body, about the lean pecs and the trim stomach, with just a suggestion of a six-pack, and she guessed he was glad with the way the traces of water glimmered on his tanned body in the light of the falling afternoon.

"You make it hard to say good-bye," he said as he dropped the towel to the floor and sauntered toward the bed.

When she got back, she knew Drew wanted to say something, but knew he wouldn't. He never could. He was up in the studio again. Maybe he was still complaining to himself about the magazine. He could do that. She was sad for a minute, thinking about him, behind that shut door. She was sad coming back. Smearing low-fat cream cheese on her low-carb bagel, she realized she had been sad a lot coming back. Drew, perhaps opportunely, came downstairs for a cup of coffee. He didn't say much or anything, really. A few specks of paint glittered around the lines of his forehead. Those lines deepened, like black scars, when he lifted his eyebrows in some silent exaggeration as he poured the tiny granules into his cup.

The deep-throated hum of the microwave. It filled the air. Maybe it somehow bore the weight of that crushing silence.

She suddenly wanted to cry.

Lucy wasn't used to crying. She wasn't even used to wanting to cry. Tears were one of the things she had given up a long time ago. You were supposed to smile when you danced, or have your face set into some soft impassivity, as the rest of your body grooved to the music. And she would never have wanted to cry dancing. Once, just before she was about to get up on the stage the first time on the tour with Da Biz, she had teared up just a little at the fact that she was actually a pro, but that was it.

As a model, she had mastered that sort of slanting inaccessibility, that kind of public, teasing intimacy that photographers so loved. She knew how to make her face cold, edgy, steely, fierce. She could set her muscles as a challenge to the viewer: I'm in my own place. That's how Minkoff, at the agency, had once put it: "The commercial model invites her looker in. She's *friendly*. But fashion, but art, demands distance. You're not some cheap tramp with her legs wide open.

It's all held in. Don't come any closer! But maybe you can hint...*just maybe*..." And then he would laugh, that high, pinched, bubbling German laugh.

So she had known how to set her face, and maybe it had become habit. But, over the past few weeks, that habit grew more distinct to her. It was like the habit was a mask, and she realized that it was there for the first time. It was stiff and rigid and sterile. As she tried to feel it, even the slightest touch revealed some alien curve. Yes, it was a mask.

The tears were not the only new thing in her life. When she left, even when she wasn't going to see Cal, she sometimes felt porcupine prickles all over her skin. They would multiply with each step as she'd walk to the front door. She'd start to say things.

"Just going out."

"Oh."

Poke.

"Meeting Kim for coffee."

"Oh."

Poke.

"Consultation for a photo shoot."

"Oh."

Poke.

Some times it was worse than others, whether what she said was true or not. Sometimes, the needles seemed to be dipped in fire. Now and then, a story would suddenly rise up and pop in her mouth, like bubbles in champagne. "I thought I was going to be back sooner, but I had a burrito at one of those street-vendor stands, and I didn't feel good at all." None of that was true. None of it needed to be said. They were just flailing words. Sometimes, she thought she told those lies (and eventually she could call them lies) as a way of trying to provoke some truth, as a way of showing, however indirectly, that some verity was still there.

It hadn't always been like this. Before, it had been easy. It had been cool and thrilling. Drew, for all his petty grasping neediness, had had a name. He was sharp, edgy, and in possession of invites to the best parties. And there had been something there in his eyes and in his voice and in his touch. She remembered walking down Flatbush, his impulsive taking of her hand and her thrill of conquest, of binding that man's floating desires. The pops of champagne and glitter of crystal. The newspapers and magazines—with her picture, with theirs. One trophy after another, and she perhaps had been the greatest trophy of them all. That's what she had said to Kim years ago, and she had laughed when she said that and felt the throbbing cry of triumph reach up through her throat.

She enjoyed sitting for his paintings and the applause and the admiring reviews. At first, she enjoyed the conquest of her youth over his middle age. Then the days had piled up. After a few weeks, hours, months, whenever, that triumph had gone stale. There was Drew, always hanging on the opinions of other men and women. He'd always turn from a painting with a remark about the applause it would give him. He loved awards and honors and spent far more time looking at the programs for any celebrations of him than in museums. Even going to galleries was just about talk-talk-talk me-me-me. At a certain point, she couldn't pinpoint exactly when, it got cold and lonely being in the trophy case. It always seemed like he was looking at her through the eyes of other people: how her body was hot to them, how they might like to roll in the sheets with her. Sometimes, when he touched her, it seemed as though his hands were another man's. And then there really was the touch of another man.

Oh, she could still play her part, and she had thought that that occasional performance would be enough. And maybe it had been, but it wasn't anymore.

She sat a few times for *work #9*. More than she had perhaps ever seen him be, Drew was irritated with the work and often listless. He'd stare at her sitting in that metal chair and rake his fingers through his sparse hair. Drew had unrolled some thick paper along one wall of the studio in a scrolling testament of frustrated images and discarded sketches. One model after another—one slash after another. He had her change clothes. Again. A few more dashes of the brush. Again. Should the diagonals be a rainbow? A single color? Green? Red? Alternating black and white? How big should her own form be? A tiny figure in the corner ("the human body dominated by the weight of industrial order"), or larger, maybe even taking up much of the canvas ("perhaps the yin and yang of organic and mechanical or perhaps the body triumphant over the urban girding")?

He wasn't even satisfied with his paintings of her. "It's not rendering right. There's something...something...missing." A shake of the head. "That elbow's right. So's that knee. Hmm...what if you turned a little *that* way? Maybe *this* way. Just a little. No. No. Forget it. Forget it." He spun to look out the windows of the studio. She watched his outline against the light.

There was the tangible instant. A sudden tenderness rose in her. There he was, not posed in complaint or rigid self-importance, but pressing at something, searching. Not only tenderness, but sympathy, even empathy. Would she—would she speak? And what would she say? The silence intervened again, the silence that was always there, now.

Before, she had not known how silence could crush. She had always thought of silence as a mere absence, a vacuum for sound to fill. Now, she knew that it could be as tangible as walls—hard and firm and unyielding—that silence could be as thick as any sound.

It was worst on those nights when they shared a bed. He sometimes, more often during the last year, crashed in his studio, and she sometimes, also more recently, would just drift asleep on the couch in front of the muted TV, but not every night. He would be there beside her, and she would wonder at the world spinning in his skull. There, in the quiet darkness, their distance was more distinct. She thought about if his pulse jumped as hers sometimes did, if he had ever wanted to cry, what he felt when he saw her cross the threshold of the front hall. Questions kept whirling in her brain like drills, and she couldn't fall asleep. She would lie there in the bed and watch as the light grew grayer through the window, flushing into the dark blue of their room.

One night, he turned and woke. "You're up?" he asked.

"Yes."

"Trouble sleeping?"

"Yes."

And those affirmations were enough. Drew turned again and slept again. The silence washed up. She drowned.

Cal noticed that things were different. There were moments of vagueness that he seized upon. "What?" he would say, dismissive, abrupt, as though he would push that fog away or maybe, as she thought at one moment, try to make the fog thicker, so that she'd accept it as reality.

Once, she replied, "Did you ever think it would be like this?"

Cal shrugged. "Are you unhappy?" There was the scorn in his voice again, the sneer on his lips, like he faced someone looking for a deal on Manhattan office space.

"I don't know why you're like this sometimes, Cal."

"Like what?"

"Like the way you are."

His smile was both taunting and self-satisfied. "You seem to like the way I am enough. You're here because you put yourself here—just like me." Those words set the daggers turning. "You put yourself here."

She went with Drew to an art show later that week, for some of the new artists of the so-called SoHo Valley School. They mingled through sundry vistas of the city—skyscrapers and choked roads, aerials and underground tunnels. Like Claire Hansen's *High Finance*, which looked like it was painted while the artist hung over the roof of the Mercantile Exchange, some of the visions were from nosebleed perspectives. Some were close, and low, of the corners of sidewalks, the edges of sewer grates. Usually, Drew would be smooth, ingratiating, prickly (always *sotto voce*), or sly at those gatherings. That night, he just drifted in silence. Occasionally, he would speak (if spoken to) and carry on a facade of conversation, but it wasn't the same.

There was only one moment of engagement. Some chatterers had gathered around a new painting by

Todd Sands, which showed a corner of Columbus Park. The composition was simple: some green trees, a few square tables around which men played dominos or cards.

"Too simple," Abe Fox said with a poking disdain. "Look at those lines, that generic use of color. It's boring—that's what it is. You know, Drew, I think that these SoHoers can take nostalgia a little too far."

Dara Ting added, "It's just all so rough and so throwbackish. It's not like your work, Drew, at all, or like Betty Orstein's." Abe nodded, mumbling his assent deep in his greying goatee. "I mean, look at that figure;"—she reached out her thin finger to point at the side of one of the men playing cards—"it's outright ungainly. It's like this vortex of the trite right in the middle of the painting—some guy holding up his cards to inspect them while he plays."

"Well, the painting's trite all over," Abe said. "Stuck in the 1950s."

"I think you mean 1850s," Dara said, which provoked Abe and some of the others into laughter.

"What do you think, Drew?" Chip Poynter asked.

"It's rough around that arm there, and you see the smearing of the trees there. For its form," he said and paused. "It's alive. It's wild and free. That's what matters. It's got it."

Dara's and Abe's eyes glanced over at him. Abe lifted his eyebrows a little, almost like it was a little joke to Dara. With infinitesimal shrugs, so small that they blended into the rise and fall of their shoulders with each step, the posse loitered on to a new painting.

"Do you like it?" he asked her when they were gone.

"It's—it's different."

"Yeah." Suddenly, for some reason he smiled. "Yeah it is."

One day, she went to the aquarium with Cal. He was irritated. There were some kids on a field trip, some tours by Japanese and, Lucy thought, German groups. There was a sea lion show. The creature shot through the water, rising through the air, its skin like polished leather. The children screamed with delight. On cue, it roared at them behind the chain-link barrier. Cal laughed.

They walked the dark arcades. Against the glass, Cal's form was a shadow, as she, she reminded herself, was a shadow. She watched the fish float along like little chips of colored glass in the great aquariums. The eels slithered inscrutably in the blue light. Crabs scuttled along, sometimes waving their claws in warning or invitation. Limbs dangling out, the octopuses pumped in the dim-lit water.

A guide came up to the glass, followed by a trailing cloud of tourists. "And here are the octopi," she began in a voice that reminded Lucy of the wire of a clothes-hanger (thin, insistent, contorted as it reached through her nasal passages). "They come in a vast variety of species, reaching back hundreds of millions of years. In hunting they use their eight arms to hold on to prey and their little beaks to devour them.

"For the most common suborder of the octopus, the *Incirrina*, the beak is the only hard part of the creature. As such, the octopus is exceedingly flexible and tenacious. Its muscular body allows it to slip through even the smallest openings. That octopus there has been recorded moving its whole body through a hole no bigger than a silver dollar. It can exploit the slightest crack, the smallest weakness. Any opening." She turned around, smiling. "And then it strikes."

The crowd drew closer against the glass. Cal walked on.

He didn't say too much. He examined a number of the creatures in silence, his eyes probing all their different qualities, like a predator or machine would. Cal admired the sharks. She could tell that from the way he nodded, his chin just a little upraised, as he watched the armada of fins and teeth float in front of him. But he grew bored and wanted to leave. She let him, and wandered the dark halls alone.

As the afternoon wore on, the crowd lessened. Her footsteps echoed a little. They reminded her of splashing water. She saw people standing up against the tanks, saw their outlines against the glowing aquamarine glass. She felt like she was walking in a world of silhouettes. So thin, so thin. In that liquid neon world, her pulse seemed like a thin trail of flame. It burned. There was her heart somewhere, that heaving source. Within that army of shadowy veneers, passing in the dark avenues, her pulse had a trembling urgency. If only she could break free, if only she could just give over to that flame. It ignited; her head swirled in fire, feverish.

The lights flickered in her eyes as she walked. *Clop clop clop.* The sounds of her steps returned to her, like growing waves. *Clop clop clop.* It just seemed so tight, the darkness. She made it to the glass doors. The open air compounded her dizziness. She sank down to the ground. Her heart was drumming in her ears, like each flicker of the flame was the pound of a thousand mallets.

One day, she didn't return Cal's call. She just hadn't bothered to pick up the phone and then she couldn't bear to call him back. The next day, he tried twice. She sat beside the phone. It didn't seem very hard not to answer. Again, the next day. And then there were no more calls. She didn't want to talk, not to him. She wanted...she wanted...she wanted something.

She would still go out, and Drew would still hurt. But how could she tell him that she had not gone to kiss another man? Not after everything. Not when she didn't even know why she did anything anymore.

One day, she went up the stairs to the studio. It had rained a little the night before; raindrops huddled along the cames. They seemed so fragile on their thin perches.

Drew was there. He had pulled out a lot of his works—from his earliest realist sketches from art school to some of his most recent mixed-media mash-ups—and scattered them around the studio. "Hey."

"Hey."

"Thought I'd look at some of the stuff." He held out his arms and gestured to the assembled works.

"It's quite a range."

"Yeah." Drew nodded and kept looking at one wall. Lucy walked around, scrutinized some of his art. There was a charcoal nude; two gray lines topped by a triangle meant to give a suggestion of the Empire State Building, guitar strings snaking up the middle; broad smears of color, shaped like a woman riding a bicycle, her hair flying like a comet's tail; various bars of color (were they a graph, a skyline—were they just bars of color?); cereal boxes framing an image of a porno mag. There was her face in profile above the cityscape; there were her eyes peeking over some fence; there was her body, hands suggestively posed in the form of modesty; there were sketches of her, in all those different pos-es—in ink and pencil, crayon and pastel, paint and watercolor. She walked through the pile of art, amidst the scattered images of herself.

"I could paint anything," he said. It wasn't a boast; there was a tightness of regret in his voice. "Any form, any style. I could get it just right. One of my teachers once called my work faultless. For some reason, that made me happy then."

"Did you think it would be like this?"

"Could it be different?" he asked in reply. "I've thought about that a lot recently. It never—I never—it's not right. Maybe somehow—maybe somehow it could be." He looked up at her, then to the windows. He was older then than she had ever seen him. With the slope of his neck and the crinkling around his eyes at that moment, he had never looked younger.

"Drew," she said, and stopped at the threshold of that word. What else could she say? What had it been for her to say the word—his name—like that? Why did it feel like she was saying his name for the first time? Something rose up at first, vast in the fog, and then receded.

Drew had to meet with a client; she had to meet Kim for coffee.

When she sat at the small table at the coffee shop with Kim, her head was swirling. "What's up, Lucy? You look different."

"How?"

"I don't know. Just different."

"I don't know, either," Lucy said. She sipped her latte and tried to concentrate on its taste. "Remember dancing, Kim?"

Perhaps caught a little off guard, Kim replied, "Sure I remember. I remember the day you came knocking on my door about the ad for a roommate. Fresh off the bus from—where was it again?"

"Swans. Swans, Ohio. I always wanted to dance." She had danced as a little girl, bouncing in her slippered feet in front of her parents' record player. Foot after foot in time with the pounding music, hands waving, sweat spilling down the sides of her face in tiny rivulets. "Remember that tour: you'd dance for like at least three hours a night, plus rehearsals, plus new routines. But, every morning, when I woke up, I was ready for more. It was like I could dance forever." She sighed. "Things weren't wrapped up with a bow back then. Maybe that bow's just a rope to tie you up."

Now Kim laughed. "Girl, you got a pretty good deal right now. And I don't know tied up you have to be. I mean, your husband, he...Well, *Drew?*" Her voice arched like steepled fingers—appraising, sardonic.

"That's different, too," she said. Just saying that, just hearing the way Kim said her husband's name, was like a handful of snow shoved down the back of her neck. And it was true, maybe, maybe it was, in a thousand ways. All her energies concentrated in a sudden moment of urgency. Maybe that was what a contraction felt like—a quick squeeze that filled you up.

Though she loved gossip (Lucy had known that ever since their days in that crumbling building in Alphabet City), Kim didn't pursue that point. She just shrugged and stirred her coffee. Soon she was talking about her new baby-sitter.

But the urgency stayed with Lucy. It grew hot within her as she walked the city streets. Yes, there had been a change. The silence had taught her things. She had learned an aware loneliness. She had learned what it meant to want to cry. She had learned—really learned—crying, there, in the afternoon at the aquarium, the hot tears streaming down her face as she sat crumpled on the cement.

Crossing a street and turning a corner, she came to a park, one just like the painting, the one Todd Sands had done. There were the men, speaking Chinese, huddled over their little tables. There was life, and it was going on. Sands must have painted the park on a day like this (if it weren't impossible, she would have said on *that* day), with the leaves catching the light and the wind stirring the stray hairs of the nannies and mothers.

She had learned sympathy or something. There was that private moment of opening. She had known the walls of silence, yes, but, perhaps, she had also known that there was something beyond those walls. Had she always known that? Were those little pricks, those anxious hurts, signs of something, of an awakening feeling for that man she called her husband? Perhaps. And perhaps there was something deep and wondrous in that sometimes pathetic, irritable, and cringing man.

A boy ran by, pulling his red balloon after him. The inflated sphere rode the air with little plunges. It struck her, for a moment, like the moon turning in front of the sun during a solar eclipse, like it did in those filmstrips in elementary school.

So, it seemed, an orb had turned in her own life. She had been granted a vision of her life—not as it was thought by other people but as it was lived by herself. It was like she had gained a new vista on her life, and she could see it, deeper, wider, truer than she ever had before. In a moment, something had sprung, like the octopus with its sudden iron squeeze.

And still the sphere turned, like a red eye turning. All her life, she had thought, had been restless. Always it had been seeking. And she had burned through men in that quest. From that first boy she had kissed to the first she had slept with to the second and the third until Drew and Javier and the unknown man, the one night in Vegas, and Cal. She had chased and chased, but now, she saw, only for a series of dead ends. Not because of the prizes themselves but because of her. Even as she had been taken, she had taken her husband as a trophy. She had put him on a shelf—as she had put her whole life on a shelf. She had tried to make the flame, the one she had wanted, the one reaching all the way from her thighs to her throat, a dead bauble.

There, on that day of flashing shadows, she realized that all her joys had been shallow. If she had reached fast for the moment and given herself to a sublime full faith, perhaps then she might have known the deeper waters. She had wanted that deep all her life. She had flung herself from one pair of nameless arms to another in pursuit of that deep, but always it was an embrace of emptiness. Her life had been lived in fear of the wild sea. She had mistook the wavering surface of life for the sun itself. If Drew had been dying by inches with her, she had been dying by inches with him—with herself. She had undergone, with a hollow frenzy, that minute death of self-distraction.

The boy jumped and crowed like a rooster. *Cockadoodledoo! Cockadoodledoo!*

The eye spun. A yearning rose within her, a yearning that dug further into her than any she had ever known. It seemed like there was some great mountain in front of her, and, behind it, was some tremendous glowing orb. The mountain reached so high that it seemed almost to blot out the sky ahead.

Cockadoodledoo! Cockadoodledoo!

That yearning brought a sadness, but this sadness, too, pierced deep. It was the sadness of opening a secret door, of seeing the illusions that had suffused her life.

If only she could start again. If only she could start to start. And start to start to start, and so on in an infinite train of *if*s. And perhaps she could try to climb, and perhaps that trial would be its own reward. If she could begin again.

Cockadoodledoo! Cockadoodledoo!

Drew was alone when she got back, when she walked up the stairs, when she opened the door.

He was looking at a picture on a torn page. "Look at this," he said. Up close, she saw that it was a man sitting by a river. It was in charcoal, the lines at times waving wildly. "I always liked this one. I did it in art school sometime. No one said anything about it—not compared to everything else I was doing—but I really liked drawing it. It felt, for a moment like *I* was really riding the river. It was only for a second—just as I was touching up some waves. I think about that some-times—how it would be nice to give over, let go, and just be swept along. To reach and just reach. Or maybe that sounds silly."

"No,"—was her voice really shaking?—"not at all."

"Really?" he asked.

"You need that trust."

Was there recognition in those eyes? "Is this how you thought it would be—like this?"

She said, "Remember when you were a kid, doing watercolors and drawings and stuff in school? Some-times you'd start something and have an idea for it, and it wouldn't turn out like you first thought. But that didn't mean it was bad. Maybe sometimes it got better than you would have ever thought."

"It's been so long. And I was so wrong."

"So was I."

"And now..."

"Now," she said, taking up his word. "Now...now...Maybe there's a way. Maybe it can start. Maybe, through it all, there's still something."

"It could be very hard."

"Yes."

They fell into a silence, but this was not the silence of before, not the inky black lines of strangling demarcation. This was the silence that knits together the space and time between two voices. A feeling rose within her during that silence, a feeling that, somehow, there could be a way. Somehow, they could step beyond. Somehow, they could meet the deep life, the life they had both thirsted for, that they had both feared.

This moment was a start, if she would take it. "We can try."

"Yes, we can try."

Motley Black

I had to get away. It was that simple. The joys of marriage. Ah, not for me. To see him kiss her...the consummation devoutly wished—no. Even if there was the souring, as in most cases there is, to see their joys turn to folly—not right now. Oh, I enjoyed my time there, with the sun and the trees overhead and the hours singing. It was a respite of a kind, I supposed. But that time was past, as times always pass.

So I bought a bus ticket to as far as I could go from there: Key West. I didn't know what I'd find there. I'd never been. I was sure I'd tire of it, but it is man's condition to tire. Soon enough, yet how long it seems, he perhaps even comes to tire of life, even if he doesn't know it. And he ends in darkness.

But I'd go to Key West, from sun to sun. Then maybe back to New York or Chicago or somewhere— somewhere cold. But later.

That's how I often had to live my life—from one later to the next. Perhaps men cannot bear to see past the next hilltop.

I had already made it to Los Angeles, sleeping on the bus over the night. Now, I had to change busses. The morning at the bus station was sunny, as had been the morning before that and the one before that and the one before that. Even—especially—pleasures can become tiresome. I could feel that old familiar swell of heat on my black shirt. The tourists were walking around, talking. A lot of them were on their cell phones. At the moment, the mood was on me, and I enjoyed listening to the flow of chattery bromides.

"Love you, too."

"It's a really nice day."

"Sunny out, really nice."

"Take care."

"Miss you."

"Well, you enjoy the beach."

"Great deal on these tickets."

A simple jingle-jangle, different from the one I was leaving behind. The mood retreated.

Squawking its usual gibberish (sometimes, it can even be tiring to think of analogies), the speaker above announced that my bus would be boarding. Transcontinental bus traveling can be a rather extended affair. While my ticket would take me all the way to the Keys, this bus was only going as far as Phoenix. From there, I had to get a bus to New Orleans.

I stood in line, in the middle of an inane whirlpool. Within that swirling nonsense, I felt an itch, then a prodding, at the side of my face. I looked up. As I suspected, I was being stared at, by a woman. Her eyes were like marbles—cloudy and unreflective.

"Yes?"

"So how are you today?" Even within the present inanity, her voice still rung with a particularly empty-skulled cheer.

I decided to give the polite answer. "*Good.*" I doubted that she could hear the twist of irony in those words, which made my mouth feel like a corkscrew. In a polite vein, I continued, "It's considerate of you to ask." So this politeness is a facade of lies; I knew, of course, that asking how I was involved some of the least possible consideration from this woman.

"Well, that's good to hear. I'm visiting my daughter in Phoenix. She goes to college there. It's a big trip, but it's worth it."

Hoping that this declaration would satisfy the woman's urge for personal exhibition, I didn't say anything in response to that and kept reading.

But I was not to be delivered from her questions, like thrown stones. "Whatcha reading?"

I was reading Burton's *Anatomy of Melancholy*, a tried and true friend. I told her as much.

She opened those marbly eyes in a display of understanding and, perhaps, commiseration. "So is that like a self-help book or something?"

"I do not know what it would mean to help myself. Indeed, I think that much of human misery can be traced to the conviction that we are worth being improved."

Her mouth hung open as she reverted to her habitual expression of incomprehension. I went forward to render my ticket to the bus driver, whose physique was like that of a hound dog with a smoking problem. A few tiny flaps of skin hung from a pencil-like neck sticking out of a blue collar about two sizes too big. A straggly red mustache clung to his upper lip.

Now, for perhaps the most high stakes part of the bus trip: seating. I was hoping for loneliness and solitude. I slumped into a window seat and stowed my rucksack on the seat next to me. That was company enough. As long as there were pairs of empty seats around me—and they were there aplenty when I sat down—that rucksack could stay.

As the line of people passed me in my seat, the game was on in earnest. It is a mark of the neophyte to think that sitting in the back of the bus will guarantee you an avoidance of a seat-mate, if such a fate can be avoided. No, too many people, their eyes fixed on some further horizon, hoping against hope that some revelation will reward them, the industrious, where so many others have failed, will push on past the half-filled seats nearer the front, hoping that some pair of seats, farther in the back, remains blissfully unoccupied. They are usually wrong, of course, so they are forced to fill up some other pair. Too much forward, and people are too lazy, too eager, too complacent, and you are almost assured of company. The middle, slightly forward, has much to recommend it, and it was there I made my stand.

The rucksack was key. Most people were too lazy to try to say anything, particularly if you were hostile or ignorant of them or—best of all—hostilely ignorant. So I forced my head down and stared into my old Burton. Out of the corner of my eye, I could see figures pass. Most just trudged on.

One woman stayed for a second. I clenched my jaw and hardened my attention on the book. She passed. My jaw loosened just a little bit more. I gave another look behind me. There were still some empty pairs of seats behind me. Another passed. A flicker of hope: perhaps no *company* for this leg of the trip.

As usual, my hopes were disappointed. A man came up. Past the humped zenith of middle age, his yellowish-gray hair spiked up on his balding head, he slouched in a partway-buttoned Hawaiian shirt. A silver chain snaked through the silvered coils of his chest hair. Lines creased his reddened face. "Hey, buddy, mind if I take a load off?" He gestured to my bag.

"You know, there are other seats farther down with no one in them."

He nodded, smiling. "Aw yeah, but, with the line of folks behind me, I know some of us will have to double up."

I pulled my bag off the seat and set it on the floor underneath me. He sat down with a *whoosh*. "Nice weather, huh?"

One of the things I most detest speaking about is the weather. Its innocuousness is proof of its triviality, and a sign of how man will while away his time with triviality. It—the weather—is immediately accessible. Its experience requires no sophistication, knowledge, or refinement of sensibility (whatever those are worth), making it a nice topic for polite and vulgar conversation.

Not wanting to indulge that vacuity, I didn't say anything.

He apparently mistook my principles for a sensory deficiency. He repeated, louder, "Nice weather, right?"

"It could be worse," I said. I could be sitting in the sun with a man like him on either side of me, instead of merely one side. Our circumstances are themselves a kind of weather, and dwelling so on the weather is a kind of unconscious vanity.

In truth, I longed for the rain. I yearned to see the drops trace their sad way down the windows, to watch the gray sky heavy above me. I still had miles of sunshine to go, but there would be some rain, I hoped, past Texas. At least in Florida, it often rained during the afternoon.

By the time the bus started, I had another prick for the lonely company of the rain: my new *friend* must have counted wrong, because there still were some empty pairs of seats behind us.

Busses often serve as a nest for noxious smells. Body odors, artificial scents, food stuff emanations, and bodily processes come together to forge a haze of stenches. The man sitting next to me was adding his cheap cologne to the mix; it reached through the mélange and wiggled in my nostrils. I tried to shut it out, to ignore it, but the wiggling was still there.

I looked over at him.

"So what part of this great green country are you heading to?"

"Florida."

The thinnish eyebrows popped up. "Really? We're gonna get to be good company, 'cause that's where I'm heading, too. Key West."

Certain moments of insight can turn your stomach. One might try to remind oneself of the sorry condition that is our lot in life, but that reminder can only dull so much of the sting occasioned by the realization of a particular suffering.

I tried—I often did—to ignore this suffering, as an animal caught in a trap might try to block the pain out of its mind. I focused my eyes on the book. But things—the emblems of his presence—kept scratching at my consciousness. I could just *feel* his heavy, dog-like presence next to me, invading my air, crowding the space. I traced the words of that fine misery in my head. I tried to let them fill my mind. Whenever I felt my thoughts swerve back to the side, I yanked my chain of consciousness hard in the other direction. Within a few minutes, my mental hand was raw from the struggle. *This Melancholy of which we are to treat, as in Habit, morbus sonticus or Chronicus, a Chronicke or continuate disease, a setled humor...*that heavy mouth-breathing...*not errant but fixed...*will he stop?...*and as it was long increasing...*another self-satisfied groan...*so now (being pleasant...*another...*or *painefull) growne to an habit...*that cologne—like an attar of indignity...*it will hardly be removed...*

"So?"

"What!" My tone perhaps, had sharpened at the blow of another—verbal—rebuke that his existence was to me, sitting there, on that bus, with thousands of miles to go.

"You know, I can't read on the bus. It makes my head spin."

"When there are no distractions, I find reading on the bus quite pleasant."

"I gotta be honest. I was never really into books. It's so lonely to read."

"I appreciate that loneliness. The distractions of the world hold little appeal for me."

"Well, I guess to each his own."

I always found that phrase grating. It was a kind of cognitive surrender, a hedonistic solipsism. *To each his own, do your own thing*—stop your mind from functioning and just go along with your immediate tendencies. I didn't say anything, though. I didn't *feel like it*. That thought gave me some dark amusement.

My companion leaned back his head. First, the slow breaths started. Then, a grumble began to curl in that exchange of air. Those dragging murmurs could be heard amidst the drone of the bus's motor. They were like sandpaper that had suddenly snuck down the back of my shirt's collar. Then the snores began, and the sandpaper began to drive hard against my neck. *AAAGR—he he he—AAARG AAAGR AAA-AAA-HUAAAA.*

Eventually, those snores disappeared within all the other nattering clamor of the bus. I focused on my book, and soon I was in my great black majestic sphere of solitude. One can always find the loneliness within life. It is always there. Conviviality, conversational relish, the glibness of society—all are signs of the struggle to ignore that loneliness, always lingering at your shoulder like an unwelcome stranger, one that we know too well. Perhaps, for many people, the only thing worse than a stranger is someone we know inside and out; despite all that knowledge, that patina of familiarity, there remains the hollow core of ignorance. What was a *friend*? Someone to unburden your heart to? Well, what would telling do? I did not need any more of projected narcissism, which constitutes the heart and soul of common friendship. No, if I needed to, I could stare at myself in the mirror. I did not need that refracted image of myself cobbled together into the appearance of a friend.

Those thoughts amused me as we drove. Watching the tips of the city rise ahead, I thought of the silly games of friendship and love in the woods I had left behind. I thought of the ring of fools moving their bodies back and forth as they sung their hippy-dippy songs. It was fitting, I supposed, how a man would try to make vernal bliss out of banishment—it was a model for so much else.

So much else. So the miles went. We arrived at Phoenix, and I stepped over the sleeping form of my—now, thankfully, erstwhile—companion. My ticket itinerary told me to catch a bus going to New Orleans. There were no busses going to New Orleans, as the ticket agent stolidly informed me. I was supposed to take the 2:20 going to Dallas, which would be departing in three minutes.

Little burning burrs had climbed their way up my chest to my throat by the time I had made it to the bus. The driver, who looked depressingly (though unsurprisingly) like my previous one, seemed almost puzzled when I stepped on. But he punched my ticket.

Those burrs turned to iced arrowheads when I looked down the aisle. There were no vacant rows. I stood a moment and took in the blank mob ahead of me. The vacant staring eyes. The haze of perpetual music. The glow of cellular phone screens on those engaged in the narcotic of texting. The fixed gaze of those with *good intentions* or a *social conscience*. The rock-like stares of men for whom life had to pound through a granite facade of ignorance, numbness, and indifference. I couldn't bear to sit next to that college student whose callowness was matched only by his sense of intellectual election; I couldn't stand the risk of sitting next to that woman with the trashy "romance" novel propped open on her lap (her *bourgeois* titillation would, I was sure, bring me to the point of nausea). So I took the irritation that I had borne and knew I could bear.

"My friends call me Foley," he said, extending a hand as I sat down.

"So what should I call you?"

The upper half of his jaw, along with the accompanying portion of his head, swung back in howling laughter. That nap had apparently given renewed vigor to his rough-neck jocularity. "That's a good one there, guy. GOOD ONE!" At that moment, I knew it would be a long ride.

Somehow, he took to calling me "Jay," after the first letter of my first name. I had never been called that before. It grated, as most other things about him did.

"So what you heading to Florida for?" he asked.

"Does there have to be a reason?"

"Every man gets up and does something because he

thinks there's a reason for it."

"Or an excuse."

"But he still looks at it like a reason."

"Even if he's ultimately disappointed?"

"Reasons can still be disappointing."

There was some wisdom there, I had to admit. "I wanted to leave here—that's my reason." I felt like tossing out another piece of conversational negligence. "Key West is far away."

"It's my kind of place, Key West. Great place, great place."

"I've never been."

"Me neither."

"Then how do you know if you'll like it? Experience, too, often disappoints." Oh, how well I knew that—that well-knowing was itself an inexorable process of disappointment.

"I figure I'll like it. I mean it looks so nice. And everyone says it's a great place."

"The fact that *everyone* likes it is perhaps what gives me the most pause about going."

After a few minutes of appreciated peace, he announced, "I'm retired, now. Or that's what I call it."

Not particularly caring what he was (in fact, caring more to *not* know what he was), I didn't say anything.

As I was learning, Foley treated my silence as a sign of great interest. I would come to appreciate the fact that he was a master of silences: he could make them interrogative, declarative, and exclamatory without even an instant's effort. He was like a magician in that regard. "The thing is, I used to work for this rich guy. I mean Forbes 500 rich. So one day I was there cleaning his pool, and I saw a little something I wasn't supposed to see. Something wifey's not supposed to see, either.

You know what I'm saying? You know what I'm saying?"

He took my silence as a cognitive affirmation.

"So we both know what's up, and he doesn't want me around anymore, and he wants to give me a nice payout—to help me forget. But like all rich guys, he's really cheap. So you know what he does? He says to me what would happen if I took a little slip by the pool? He's got a real nice homeowner's policy. So you see where this is going, don't ya?"

"The spoils of fraud?"

That cigarette-stained laughter, again. "I got darn tired of wearing that neck-brace, though. It took a long time for that settlement, and I was tailed for a whole lotta time. But they didn't see a thing. Not a thing."

I didn't know if he was waiting for my congratulations, but, after a moment, he repeated, "So now I'm retired."

He wanted to know what I did for work. When I told him that I, in a moment of youthful pique, had written the lyrics to a Top-40 single (I always thought of it as a nonsense song, but it appeared that most other people didn't get the joke), he was impressed. The royalties were enough to live on, if one lived frugally.

"I'm from the East Coast," I explained (somehow, I had gotten into explaining), "even if I have spent more time in the West recently. It was Seattle before the Bay Area."

"Seattle?" Foley blew out his lips in dismissal. "It's so gray and gloomy there."

"And what's wrong with that?"

"It just rains all the time."

"And that's a problem?"

"Yeah buddy."

"Our debility is shown by the fact that we prefer staying dry to being in the rain. Why should lack of wetness be preferred to drops of water? People stand in showers in the morning and then complain about a few liquid specks that afternoon. That same ocean so busy during a sunny day is suddenly abandoned because a sprinkling of water from the sky. It's habit that makes people believe that. We cripple ourselves with habit, you know."

"That sounds pretty depressing there, Jay." He leaned back in the seat, as though that mention of depression was the closing of the conversation.

It was growing dark. The lights of the cities reached in a reddish blur over the flat desert. A baby in the back of the bus was crying. Eventually, we get tired of crying and the feelings of those tears, so we block them out, or cover them with some carapace of our daily life. It is a tedious business, all that pretending.

I turned to Foley and said, "We are born with a cry, through the gates of pain. Man wakes, grows, thinks that perhaps, for him, that introductory agony was a momentary wrong. He plays and pretends his whole life away, shoving himself into different uniforms to fill the void provoked by the haunting suspicion that, somehow, his whole life is a pursuit of misdirection. We celebrate our pains to try to make them meaningful. A man has a child—a cause and victim of pain, irritation, annoyance—and he must make a show of loving it to fool himself that it is the life of the child that brings him joy. So we fill the stage of the world. Then the lights begin to dim. The velvet curtain thins. The ropes and pulleys tire. The shoulders sag, in numbness, rarely in wisdom. We end in the blanket of darkness, nullity wrapping around us. Our whole life is the path to that embrace. And, for this, one should be happy to be alive? That is the blessing and curse of the whole thing: there's no escape, except into nothing. We have to be, or *we* are no more."

He replied with a question that was as *à propos* as his comments usually were. "You ever been married, Jay?"

I could barely restrain a laugh at this question. There is a kind of rich blackness in the right kind of laugh, like rippling water in the middle of the night. "As ridiculous as I am, I am still too sober for marriage, perhaps the most ridiculous state known to man."

"Ah, it's a good way to be."

"So are you?"

The chuckle-grunts rumbled in his throat. "Ah, I can't keep a wife."

"I wonder why." That was one of those trivial comments that could amuse me, when the mood took me. The mood was inspired, perhaps, by the banality of his appreciation, the manner in which distance endeared that state to him.

"And I've tried with two of them. Too many nights in that bar, you know, coming back smelling to beat the band with a dirty old stick. I've mostly given up drinking, you know."

"I didn't."

"I say *mostly*, 'cause once in a while I enjoy one of them old benders. Almost for old times' sake. But it's good to be married. To have someone there."

"Someone to distract you, annoy you, deprecate your days with her perpetual frivolity."

"Haven't you ever looked at a woman, Jay, and thought to yourself, *I'd like a piece of that*?"

"You mean like love?"

Foley's mouth curled as his eyes rolled in consideration. "I didn't mean like that, but yeah." Words—frenetic shrugs. Maybe they were the same to him.

"Love is perhaps the one state that exceeds marriage in its folly. Love is a trap we build for ourselves. It's a noose of foolishness around our necks. I have seen what *love* can do to people. It is a kind of self-induced inebriation."

"Like that's a bad thing! I mean, the inebriation part."

"You would say that, wouldn't you?" I wondered, though, if the curve of my smile (quite unintended) in saying those words dulled the edge of my voice.

Around four in the morning, we had a stopover at a truck stop outside of Forth Worth. I hadn't eaten for hours, so Foley and I agreed to go into the 24-hour diner across the parking lot. I watched our two shadows accompany us along the way, the giant lights casting them broad around us.

There were a lot of truckers there—fat, stinking beasts in flannel and stained cotton t-shirts. Profanity flew as easily from their mouths as filterless cigarette smoke and belches. A waitress scooted us into a sticky-tabled booth. The menus felt coated with slime and grime.

"This should be nourishing," I said.

"Feels comfortable, like," Foley observed.

Two waitresses worked at the place. One—ours—stared out of a face which had been pounded against the existential pavement so many times that its expression was fixed in a kind of curdled, numb stare. Expressions of emotion never reached into her eyes or the tone of her voice. "What do you want." Her voice could not reach that height of inflection to make it sound like a question.

The other waitress struck Foley's heart. When he saw her, he bounced his sunglasses up and down on his nose (yes, he did wear them inside), crying out, "*A-woo-gah, a woo-gah!*" Her face showed the faint suggestion of tire-marks from years of smoking; with a few more decades, those lines would be etched deep across her face. But her body was trim—in a lean, white-trash kind of way—with a generous bulge for her breasts (and, I wondered, breast implants). Her hair must have just been rebleached—not a trace of roots could be seen above her brown eyebrows.

Foley kept looking at the faux-blonde waitress. Perhaps even he had to distract himself from the homely charms of the diner. There was a brown ring at the bottom of my water glass. When the meatloaf I ordered was set before me, I stared at a puddle of green gravy covering a brownish, glinting slab of meat. Cutting into this submerged meat was like cutting into a sponge. Again, I relished the joys of the road. Then I wondered why I would prefer the food of my former location to this—merely because it was supposed to *look nice*? My concerns about my fickle consideration of looks were immediately undercut by the first taste of the green-battered meat. Oh, I had reasons for my preference.

Foley ate his hockey-puck-like burger quite cheerfully, if distractedly. "You got anything for me in that plate?" he called out to the object of his interest. This was one of his many addresses to her throughout the night.

"You be a good boy and focus on cleaning your own plate," she shot back.

"I gotta get some reward for being good," he replied. There, at least, Foley demonstrated much of the human race's innate sense of virtue.

"Keep eating!"

A few minute later, Foley renewed the exchange. "So what time do you get off?"

"You got a ring for this finger?" She held up her nicotined hand.

"I don't know about a ring, but I got something for—"

I reminded Foley that it was hard enough to eat my "meatloaf" (I had taken to using quotation marks to refer to it even in my thoughts); I didn't need to taste it again coming back up. "It's ridiculous," I said to him later. "You're twice her age. And even you would get bored by her lack of polish."

"Polish? That's not what I'm interested in."

"Do you have nothing that concerns you beyond your immediate appetites?"

He shrugged. "They keep me entertained. I mean, what do we have beyond those appetites? You have an appetite for feeling miserable and putting the worst spin on everything. It seems to keep you all jollied-up."

"I face my condition as it is. It is not a matter of amusement."

"What is it a matter of, then?"

"That is my own business," I said. I was on the verge of saying something cheap or unworthy or vacuous. *"It is a matter of authenticity." "It is a matter of self-respect." "It is a matter of living."* I couldn't bear to say such silly things, even in a moment of passion, even in front of him.

I wandered over to one of the benches in the bus area and dozed for a while. A few of the other passengers from the bus were there, too. I don't know if I *slept well* or not. The phenomenon of *sleeping well* is a sign of the human drive to find achievement in everything, even—especially—the most banal. It is surprising, perhaps, that phrases such as *breathing well* or *passing gas well* or *scratching well* have not entered common circulation.

In the later morning, the next bus pulled up. Foley shook me awake, and we boarded the bus together. Though there were plenty of seats, I sat down next to him. Who could know, after all, who could get on the bus later? The new driver was rumpled and red-faced. "Alright folks, here we go," he said with a nasally drawl as we left the truck stop behind.

We were getting closer to Key West. Expectations crawled up my throat somehow, despite my intention to be indifferent, to accept the oblivion of miles. Key West would be just another momentary resting place. I chided myself at the foolish enthusiasm that the profane world can inspire. We set up idols of one destination or another when we should know (and maybe do know deep down inside) that the arrival will occasion another disappointment. The glorious horizon seen far off becomes a hollow scene once we arrive at it.

"The myth of the pot of gold at the end of the rainbow is appropriate for the tricks the world plays upon us," I remarked to Foley. "We will never arrive at it, but we keep looking anyways. It's human ignorance or stubbornness or perhaps a combination of both. Stubborn unknowing."

Foley shrugged. "But you can have a good time along the way. That's what I'm keeping my eye on. That's the potted gold right there."

"Pot of."

"Pot of gold right there. Whatever."

In Louisiana, just outside Baton Rouge, we stopped to change drivers. The new bus diver was like the Pillsbury Doughboy given a sex-change operation and

Neanderthalic twist. Her squat head swung a shining pony-tail back and forth like a flail. Lumbering into the driver's throne (for she took it like a barbarian chieftess), she gave a coronation address. "When I'm up here on this bus," she shouted, "I expect *respect, quiet,* and *discipline.* You are not to get out of your seats while this bus is in motion, you are not to address the driver unless spoken to, and you are to listen to all of your driver's instructions. And I mean all of them." Settling deeper into her plastic-lined throne, she started the bus. "I'm not afraid to throw a body off."

Our ursine leader demanded considerable silence as she drove along. Her voice flickered abrasively over the intercom. "You in the back there, quiet down." A pause. "I mean like now. We got rain coming down, and I need my concentration." Someone got up and began to walk to the back of the bus, presumably to use the bathroom. "Sir, you are not to leave your seat while this vehicle is in motion." He tried to stammer something about his bodily needs. "Sir, I will not ask you again." The unfortunate figure sat down.

Foley and I had our own misfortune in sitting closer to the front of the bus and her orbit of interest. So when Foley started to laugh at one of the driver's rebukes to another passenger, she was quick to notice. "Sir, this is not a comedy show. We must keep appropriate decorum on the bus."

When she pulled over to the side of the road for what she called a "walk stop," a few people grumbled. "I'll toss you right out of here," she snarled in response. The rain had stopped, and she got out and paced back and forth outside the bus for a few minutes. No one else was allowed to join her or even to get out of their seats. The fellow who had to use the bathroom snuck into the back. He was returning to his seat when the driver entered. She trudged up to his seat—I felt her lumbering bulk pass me like a juggernaught. Holding up a slip of yellow paper, she said to him, "This is your first demerit for disobedience. After this, you're leaving."

When the bus stopped to pick up new passengers, she would rise again. Going up and down the aisle like a stalking colossus, she would yell, "Eyes up! Eyes up!" Her shrewish eyes hunted for any infraction of her transportation dogma: bags on the seat, food, open drink containers, people on cell phones, headsets turned on too loud (anything she thought she could hear). Most of these rules were the ferment of her pugnacious and bored mind; only flight attendants exceed bus drivers in their combination of those two qualities.

At one stop, a man was shaking his head in bemusement at the present situation.

"Is there a problem, sir?"

"No. It's just that this is pretty crazy." His words stumbled over some fizzing laughter.

"Well, then, you can leave."

The man held up his hand. "No, I'm fine."

"Sir, that wasn't a request."

"But I—" he was saying as she escorted him off the bus.

"You'll have to just wait for the next bus."

So the bus drove off and left him behind.

"This is exciting," Foley whispered to me.

"The abuse of power often is, especially when its stakes are so mean."

We drove, and the rains began again. The world seemed to be tapping on that little capsule of bureaucratic terror we rode in.

Foley was speaking with another passenger in front

of me. I was deep into Burton, so I failed to hear the palaver in detail.

"Let's keep it down back there," the driver growled over the intercom.

"So she said, 'Drop and give me twenty!'" Foley whispered to the fellow ahead of him. Both passengers ahead of us broke into a flood of laughter, which swept Foley into a laughing fit (he always had the tact to laugh—usually the loudest—at his own jokes).

The bus swerved as it lurched to the breakdown lane. "You pushed me too far," she crowed. And then, I could hear it: her bulk moving to stand up.

"Eyes up! Eyes up!" I could almost hear the spittle flying from her mouth at this frantic invocation. I heard her steps. I kept my eyes on Burton. "Eyes up!" Even I could face only so much of this absurdity.

"Now, I been patient. And maybe I been too patient. You let a hen start pecking, it'll peck itself to death. You over there"—I could hear that voice getting louder as she came closer—"have been giving me trouble since day one. And—SIR!"

I could feel those sound waves lap against my face. I looked up to see her eyes like black coals burning through layers of fat.

"Did you not hear me demand your eyes up?"

"Well..."

"Answer me that!"

I replied that I would answer nothing with a tone like that.

"See, this is what I'm talking about." This observation was apparently meant for the whole bus. "It seems we got some *nonconformist* here who thinks he can just sink his nose into a book in complete disregard of the *rules*. Well, here we are. Sir, I'm going to have to confiscate that book."

"For what purpose?"

"It is an instrument of insubordination."

I felt the black laughter rising up in me again. "Now, that's a pretty phrase."

"Sir, the book."

I refused to honor that demand with a verbal reply.

"Give me that book, or I will tase you."

I looked up at her bull-pig face. "Madame, I am quite certain that you will *not* tase me. The legal ramifications alone..."

"Sir, on this bus, I AM the LAW."

"Madame..."

"Sir, I done tased a body before, and I will tase a body in the future if there is a single instance of insubordination that impairs my effectiveness as a driver."

"Madame, I fail to see how me reading my book will impair your driving capacities."

"Sir, it is your persistent lip that undermines my ability to devote sufficient, secure attention to the other passengers."

"Do you even know what that means?"

"Sir, now you done it..."

"Hold on, hold on here!" Foley cried as he stood up. It was like he was the only person on the bus other than myself and the driver who had any cognizance of the conversation. (In that moment of interruption, I saw the eyes of the other passengers staring off blankly ahead.) "Can't we—"

"This is like insubordination city!" the driver hollered, almost as though she were trying to unite the other passengers behind her in sympathy. "We got a whole-hog rebellion going on here!" Perhaps the shock of revolution shook the thought of the taser out of her mind. "Sir," (to me) "I'm going to have to ask you to leave."

"Right now?"

"Right now."

"At the side of the road, in the rain?"

"You got that one right, Mr. Smartypants."

A few minutes later, I stood on the side of the highway, my rucksack slung over my shoulder. The bus pulled away.

Foley was with me. He had refused to let me go off alone. Se we stood there together in the rain.

"Well, Foley," I said, "shall we go?"

"Let's go."

The rain falling on us, we walked farther down the road.

Dunes Like White Elephants

The beach along the Sequanesett Bay was long and yellow-white. The man walked with stiff knees, almost as though they were surprised at the earth or surprised that they would bend. The woman pulled her sweater a little closer to her body as she walked. Even though it was late afternoon, the sun had not yet baked the sand. It was gritty and edged with a bit of the winter's earlier chill.

"Look at those dunes," the woman said.

"Like frozen waves," the man replied.

"They're almost like the backs of elephants—of white elephants."

"Is there such a thing as a white elephant?"

"Yeah, I think."

"Oh."

The woman continued, "They're so big, big and heavy in the horizon. Kind of like storm clouds."

"Except on the ground."

"Yeah, except for that, I guess."

The sea tossed up a few pieces of seaweed, which lay glistening on the water's edge.

"You're sure?" he asked.

"I'm sure I'm sure."

"Yeah, I know." He bent his head. "So?"

"So?"

"I mean, I mean, it's not like we're kids."

"No." She stared out at the water, as it swept the bits of seaweed into its maw and sent them tumbling forward again. "We can't ever be kids again." She turned toward him. "That's strange, isn't it?"

"Maybe it is, I guess."

She pointed. "Look at that seagull."

The bird flew above them. It settled on the water with a tiny splash. Then, its gray-and-white wings folded, and it bobbed along with the waves.

"It can go from one place to the other so easily," she said. "From the sky to the water to the beach. Does it have any kids, you think?"

He shrugged. "How would I know? Should I ask? My seagull's a little rusty..."

"You're being silly."

"Really?"

"That's not a decision you can erase, you know," she said.

"Being silly?"

"No. Not that."

"So maybe it isn't."

"It's just—so sudden." She swallowed.

"Yeah."

A couple walking their dog passed them. The little steps of the canine stood out like indents of starfish in the sand.

"Hi."

"Hello."

"Good afternoon."

They walked with only the crashing of the waves for conversation.

"Would it be real?" she asked.

"Real?"

"You know, not just playing?"

"I think we're past the point of games," he said.

"Yeah. I guess so."

They paused. The woman picked up a rock, worn

smooth by the waves. She ran her finger over its cool, dry surface. She clutched it in her hand. "What would our families think?"

"Of course they'd be happy."

"You don't know my parents that well."

He shrugged. "But they like me, don't they? I mean, enough."

"Enough for what?"

"You get the point. But do they?"

She said, "They don't complain about you."

"See?"

"And I've never met yours."

"I know they'd love you," he said.

"Why?"

"You're a very lovable person."

"Oh."

They resumed walking. "There, you're smiling—you're smiling. You don't need to hide it, you know."

"You can still make me smile."

He smiled. "I guess."

"You still have your charm."

"Charm?"

"Charm."

She took the rock and tossed it whirling through the air. It splashed through the water with a burst of white foam, as it peeled apart the upper layer of the sea. Then the waves washed over that opening again. The sandy depths held the stone.

"Do you think it would be a bad idea?" he asked.

"No. I mean, not necessarily. It's just—" She paused, looking out to the sea. "It's just that we haven't known each other very long."

"How long do you really need to know someone—you know, before you really know?"

"Would you want to do this—without, well, this?"

"What kind of question is that?"

"A serious one." She kept walking.

"We can't change the past," he said, following.

"No. Things can't be like they were before."

"But is that really the worst thing?"

"Maybe not. Things have to change, don't they?"

"Yeah," he said, "they do."

"I'm cold." She tugged on her sweater.

"Yeah, the wind is pretty fierce," he said.

A few grains of sand tumbled through the air. They kept walking against the wind. The woman's hair whirled out in fits of curls.

She said, "I just don't know." She shook her head. "It's kinda scary."

"I don't want you to do it if you're scared."

"Who said I was scared?"

"I thought you did."

"Things can be scary, and you don't need to be scared by them," she said.

"Oh."

"What, you don't believe me?"

"It's just..."

"Just what? And what if I were scared—wouldn't that be normal? Just to be—just a little scared?"

"Well..."

"It's easy for you to talk about it."

"Hey," he said, "wait a minute. It's not like I'm not involved here, remember? It's not like we're both not involved."

"No, I—I guess we are."

"And, yeah, it's different for me. But it is still my life. And yours."

"And our—" She took a breath. "We're not alone in this."

"But maybe I'm a little scared, too."

"Just a little?"

"Whatever happens, happens. And that's it." He slipped his hands in his pockets. "So I guess I don't want you doing this if you're *too* scared."

"And you're not *too* scared?"

"No. No I am not."

She rested her hand on her belly. "This world's crazy."

"Yeah, it is."

"You're not even going to try to argue about that?"

"At a certain point, I guess it doesn't really matter. We're in the craziness, after all."

"Yeah."

"And maybe it's not completely bad."

"Maybe."

He smiled. "There are good things in life."

"You're like out of a memory when you say that."

"What?"

"Oh, I don't know." The wind had blown some of her hair across her face, so she reached up and pulled it to the side. "What if we're wrong, and we look back and just regret everything?"

"So we do."

"That's comforting."

"We might have regrets no matter what. We won't know."

"No, we won't."

"But, you know, we might also look back and be happy. I know that sounds crazy."

"Stop," she said.

"OK."

"I guess the answers don't get easier."

"No, I guess not."

"It's a big change."

"At a certain point, you know," he said, "it's either death or life. That's what it comes down to."

"I know I know I know I know."

"And we just can't pretend—"

"I know."

A few seagulls wheeled overhead. She stopped and looked at the beach ahead of them, with its curves and jetties and hidden inlets.

She said, "I'll lose my figure, you know."

"I never really cared about your figure. I mean, just about your figure."

"That's sweet."

"That's true," he said. "I might go bald."

"That doesn't matter to me."

"I'll keep that in mind."

"You know what I mean."

"Yeah, I guess I do."

The waves rolled and the sun continued its downward slope in the sky as they walked. The sky's color changed, as it grew more and more flushed with a red-purple hue. They passed a few people and waved each time. The dunes still reached into the distance in a long train. From the grasses, bugs began to chirp. Their intermittent calls resembled the faintest beating of a heart.

She didn't say anything for a long time, even after they had turned back. The man walked, looking at her over the space in between them.

"So," he asked, "what—how are you?"

"I'm fine, I'm fine, I'm really fine."

Billy Stevens Is 28

Billy Stevens at an otherwise empty table at the coffee shop. It's a quiet morning, with only a few other patrons lounging around.

The front door opens: Samantha. There is, perhaps, a tightness to her face, a rigidity in the way her foot hits the ground. Billy's smiling as she sits down. "Hey," he says.

"Hey."

"I didn't order anything yet. Thought I'd wait for you. So, what, ah—"

"Don't worry about it." She sets her purse down on the table. "I don't." Her brow crinkles just a little as she says this, even as there's a ripple in her voice. A breath in. "This is harder than I thought it would be."

"What?"

"This." She puts her hands on the table. "We've had some great times. And you're a really great guy. You should know that."

"Sam—a..."

"Billy, this isn't working out." The ripples grow in her voice. "And it won't."

"Oh."

"It's not you. Really, I mean really, it isn't. You're a great guy. A thousand girls would be lucky to have you. So would I—if I was the right girl."

"And you just—you just decided this?"

She brushes at her face, around her eyes. "I woke up one morning, and I knew. It was like this cold hand inside my chest. I tried to ignore it. I really tried. But I couldn't, you see. I couldn't."

"Oh."

"I just knew. I just knew there was something—something—missing. I thought I was wrong. I kept trying to tell myself—but this isn't right. Do you see that?" She reaches forward and takes his hand. "We really did have some good times, didn't we, Billy?" She smiles, and the web of wrinkles rises for an instant. "It's okay to be sad, you know. I'm probably gonna cry all night." She sniffs—like the scratch on a matchpad. "I probably shouldn't have said that."

"Ah," he says, and then there is silence, between these two people in the coffee shop crowd. He looks at the contrast of his skin against the little brown and gray and green specks of the table. She looks—anywhere.

"I still love you, Billy, and I still care for you. And I'll always be here for you. You know that, right?" She looks into his eyes, blinks her own and looks away.

He nods. "I do." He pauses. "So is this it?"

"Good-bye, Billy Stevens." One more pat on the hand, and then she rises. "Good-bye." Her shoes click on the floor. With a slight *ring*, the glass door shuts behind her.

Billy sits in his chair for a few moments, unmoving. Then he gets up and walks over to the counter.

"One latte, please—medium."

***

Tuesday.

The alarm goes off at seven. *Bleep bleep bleep bleep. Blear blear blear blear.* Billy Stevens gets up every day because he gets up every day. As usual, he showers, shaves, lifts his free weights about five or ten times, wraps some geometric tie around his neck. He grabs a Pop-Tart for breakfast and is out the door. As usual, his roommate isn't up; that day, as with most days, Ross won't get up until noontime.

He sits in his cubicle, tries to type on his laptop. There's a feature for the Sunday section. But it is only Tuesday. Ah, Tuesday.

"Stevens," the sports editor calls out to him. "We got a girls volleyball game tonight. You're up. I'll want two hundred words by eight pm. And get me those score boards."

"Got it," Billy says. So he scans the wire service. He has an interview with a local football player, sometime.

"Find out something interesting," the editor tells him.

"I'll try," Billy mumbles to himself. He almost breaks out laughing.

He keeps looking at the clock. It hypnotizes him sometimes. Even when he's busy, he'll shoot a quick glance. Yeah, time just keeps on turning, the clock winding down. To what?

Lunchtime. He walks down the streets, grabs a hot dog from a sidewalk vendor. It's kinda lukewarm. Chew chew chew.

The afternoon goes on. Tick tick tick.

Balancing his laptop on his knees (the high school gym doesn't have any press tables), he types during the game. The girls scream with a score. A few of the parents swear—not at the ref, just at the world.

"You know," one audience member says to another. "They all talk about how Melissa's going to get some scholarship for volleyball."

"She's not that good."

"You know, I didn't think so, either. But, you know, that's what happens when your daddy's best friends with the coach; you get all the advantages."

"Tell me about it."

Billy feels lonely as he watches the cheering victors and even the stolid losers. They seem to have hope in their eyes—or life or something.

Later, after work, hitting up the bar with Ross. One-dollar beers on Tuesday nights.

"What are we doing here?" Billy asks after his first beer.

"What we do every Tuesday?" Ross replies. He drops a few coins in the jukebox. Guns N' Roses.

"Oh yeah."

Ross laughs. "Come on, bro, lighten up! You know what your problem is, Billy?"

"What?"

"You take life too seriously." He flashes a V-sign toward the bartender. "Hit us up, baby. Dos."

Billy makes it partway through the trivia game before he gives up. Ross tries to chat up a girl or two.

The bar winds down and the boys stagger home. The moon rises, an ice-white globe above them. Billy feels certain cold pricks through the numb, mildly flushed haze of his face.

"I don't know, Ross," he confesses, "I just don't know."

"Know 'bout what?"

"'Bout everything. I mean, do you know how long we've been doing this? How long we've been here?"

"Twenty-eight years. That's how long we've been living, breathing, bleeding, drinking—"

"Don't tell me about it..." He swallows down a spurt of cold. "My life, my life, my life." It's a despairing stutter.

"Oh your life," Ross slurs. He sounds almost giddy. "You try to make a big deal out of everything."

"Shouldn't my life be a big deal? Like why am I breathing!?" Billy drags his feet along the sidewalk, listens to the *scuff scuff scuff*. It sounds heavy. "It's like something's missing, like in here." He punches his chest. "It's cold."

"I know. Fall's here."

"It's like I was supposed to get on some train, and I never even made it to the station." His feet step higher, his steps grow more wild, more fierce against the pavement. "It's like the same thing every day. It's like I'm stuck and have to keep ordering pepperoni pizza day after day after day. And maybe I don't want pepperoni. Maybe I want onion."

"ONION! ONION! ONION!" Ross crows to the sky. His voice gallops up the facades of buildings.

"Maybe I don't even want pizza. Maybe I want to live."

Ross swings close, hangs from Billy's shoulders. "And what would living be?"

"I don't know that anymore, either."

They keep walking. Ross sings a little. "*Oh wake oh wake! Awake awake!...Oh moonlight and ecstasy! Oh moon, oh moon, speak to me! To me to me to me!...Click clack...look who's back...I'm in love, I'm in love, I'm in love!...It's me!*"

The two compatriots make it up the stairs with only a few slips and stomps. Ross is able to pick up the mail on the way in (even if he does drop it all over a landing in mid-trip). They enter the apartment in darkness. Billy tumbles face-down onto the futon-couch. Ross slumps onto the floor.

"How long have we been living here—"

"I told you: twenty-eight years."

"Seriously."

"Your problem again."

"I mean here, like *here*."

"Like *here*," Ross repeats.

"It was after college..."

"...before today..."

"...right after I moved to the *Standard*..."

"...that Cinco de Mayo party we had wasn't busted last year..."

"...but the year before th—five. Five years."

Ross stretches. "The good times go fast. What?"

"Nothing. Nothing."

"You tired of this place?"

Billy shrugs. "Well, we have been here a while."

"We could always move when the lease comes up."

"And where would that get us? I mean we could, but, it's like, what's the point? We'd just be someplace else. Some other *here*."

"You make that sound like a bad thing."

Billy says, "I mean, here I am living with my sophomore roommate from college."

"And you don't bring me flowers anymore."

"Dude, I mean, it's not you. It's just like nothing's changed, that's all, in my life. You know, I think habit's the only reason why I get out of bed in the morning."

"Or why I get out of bed in the afternoon." Arching his back, Ross yawns.

"But it's not supposed to be like that."

"What's it supposed to be like?" Yawn. "Spaceships and rainbows and princesses?"

"I don't know. I don't know."

Ross rises from the floor and crosses to the fridge. "Trust me. You're just a little drunk and a little bummin' about, you know, what happened with Samantha. Soon enough, things'll be right back to normal." He inspects the beer bottles, the carton of orange juice, the few fragments of relish in neon green juice.

"My normal's my problem. And the thing is, I wasn't even sad, I'm not even sad about the whole Sam thing. You know what I felt when she broke up with me?"

"What?" No way he could eat the relish.

"Nothing, nothing, nothing. It was just like a blink or something."

"Ahh..." Ross walks back into the living room.

"I almost wish I felt. Hurt, like really hurt, like my heart cracked into a million little pieces or something. At least then I'd know it was there."

"Ah, Billy, ah Billy," Ross says as he looks for the remote in the gray. "Poor dreamer."

"Like I still have dreams."

Ross flips on the TV. Its waving blue light fills the room, washes over Billy's smushed face. A close-up of a woman's hand slicing tomatoes.

"Infomercials," Ross says, "my favorite."

The images flash on the screen, the sound muted.

"The food looks so much better with the sound off," Ross observes. "It's very Zen, you know, to watch the TV in silence; by taking away, you get more back."

"It didn't use to be like this."

"No?"

"No. There were days when I woke up and I was on fire." Billy stares at the waving light of the TV on the floor. "Or it seems that way now. Maybe that's all there is: disappointed memory."

Ross belches. "That's poetic. You have had too many beers."

"Is that all you think it is?"

"No. No. But for *you* to be talking that way, you must be drunk."

Billy says, "Oh, I see."

"Let me tell you a story, Billy. Way back in my younger days—we're talking high school here—there was this pretty girl in the chess club; she'd just transferred in. Now, I don't know what she was doing in the chess club, but there she was. So I smile at her over the chess pieces for a few weeks, let her checkmate me a few times. You know, keep her interested. So I ask her out, and you know what she says?"

"No?"

"She says *yes*. Now I had thought about dating her lo those many hours at the board. And you know how long we lasted?"

"No."

"Ten days. No fireworks. No wild fling. Only boredom. That's when I figured out why she was in the chess club. I bet she thought I was boring or crazy or something, too. That's where expectation got me. Disappointment. The best part of our relationship was, I assure you, in my head."

"Oh."

Silence. The knife moves on to apples. They fall in slices, too.

Ross scratches his bushy hair in appreciation. "Now that's a skillful cutaway. Real art right there. Look at the smile on that woman's face. Real happiness, too. And maybe this is it. Just this. No trains or airplanes or dragons."

The silence returns. A new product appears on the screen. It's a waxing agent—from cars to countertops. The bearded MC wipes it on one surface after another. The camera picks up the audience's applause.

"That was a long time ago," Billy says.

The silence again.

"Man, I'm like starving," Ross says. "You wanna get

a pizza? La Familia delivers until three."
"Yeah, sure, maybe, yeah."

***

Reunion.

The ballroom at the local Marriott. They had held
the prom here, ten years back. Red and white crepe
paper streamers hang from the ceiling and drift a little
with the exhaust from air vents. A disco ball slowly
rotates above. Songs from the mid-nineties yawn out of
the speakers by the DJ.

Billy Stevens is there. A few people rib him about
the tie.

"You look good," Jake Shire says. In the past ten
years, Jake's shaved his head and put on about fifty
pounds. He now looks like a giant florid bear.

Suzanne Langley, who swore she'd never have kids,
shows Billy picture after picture from her digital camera of her three rugrats, aged five, three, and newborn.

Kip Marin's now a lawyer; Dave O'Hara, a fireman;
Liz Schultz, a teacher. "Sports? You do sports? Guy's
dream right there," Kip says, knocking him on the
shoulder with that shiny good-old-boy laugh. "What I
wouldn't give to be doing that. It's a lot more exciting
than contracts."

"Yeah," Billy says.

Principal Adler's even there, still in his bow tie, still
with his balding head (a few strands sweeping across
the top). "Like the tie, Billy."

"Yeah, well I got into wearing it for work." A few
more good pumps of Adler's hand. "Man, you haven't
changed a bit. You look the same as well—since forever."

"I'll take that as a compliment."

"That's how I mean it, Principal Adler." He is still "Principal Adler" to Billy.

"You still have that look, Billy, the look of the guy who ran his underwear up the flagpole." That had happened, when the review board had come and saw plaid flapping in the breeze. The Billy of those days did stuff like that.

"Do I, do I really?"

"Well..." The principal demurs. Billy tries to keep smiling.

"So you still keeping the kids in line?"

A smile reaches beneath the black-rimmed glasses. "I try, you know. Show them wisdom, virtue, respect for duties."

"I'm sure you do."

"Reunions are always interesting, I find. You see how men and women change—or don't change. How their choices matter. When you first plant a seed, everything's together and anything could grow anywhere, but, with the passage of time, the seed spreads and opens and reaches out. Tips of a plant that had been together stretch with time so that they will never touch again."

"But things can grow together, too, in time, can't they?" Billy asks.

"Oh of course they can. Who knows what will happen with time? But time persists, you see, and our choices, for good or ill—well, they count, too. And so it goes on and on and on."

"You use that whole seed metaphor a lot, don't you?"

"I try to get it in at least once a reunion."

Through the dull crowd, Michelle. Yes, that is her.

"It was great to catch up, Principal Adler," Billy says,

taking the principal's hand again, "but there's someone I, ah, I was hoping to see."

"Good luck."

Billy's train of thought catches itself on that phrase for an instant before he continues his push through the crowd.

She's more beautiful now; it's the beauty of before, magnified. Her golden hair still has that slight curl, the one he'd love to run his fingers through. "Michelle?" he says to her.

"Billy!" she cries out. "Billy Stevens!" They hug in greeting. "Fancy seeing you here," she says.

"Yeah," he says, "yeah."

"So what have you been up to?"

"Well, I cover sports for the *Standard*, so if you ever need any tickets to a little league game, I'm the guy to call."

"I'll have to keep that in mind." Her lips bend in amusement along with her voice.

"And how've you been?"

She smiles and shrugs—very pretty, very graceful. "Oh, I'm fine."

"So I heard you were doing something in New York City?"

"Yeah. Urban access to healthcare. I work for a nonprofit."

"Very—ah—noble. How'd you get into that?"

"Well, during college, I interned at this one place, and one thing led to another, and I just stayed on."

"Nice," he says.

There's a momentary pause. It seems quiet, even though Billy knows that there's music going on. It's just nice to see her.

He holds out his hands in happy astonishment.

"Man, you look great. I mean, you always did, so it's no surprise or anything."

"C'mon."

"I mean it. You know, I always thought you were the prettiest girl in high school." She starts to protest. "I did. I really did."

Michelle smiles, teasing. "How come you never asked me out, then?"

"'Cause you were the prettiest girl in high school." He takes a breath. "I mean, I thought about it, like a lot. But I guess I never could pull the trigger." He pauses, swallows. "Wow—ten years."

"Yeah. It's been a while."

"That dress looks really nice on you." It does. Red and tighter up top while looser by the legs. The fabric sways with her steps, with her tiniest motion. Its edge plays along her knees, sweeping smoothly.

She reaches down to run her hands along the side and front. "Thanks." She smiles, broad as she holds out her arms. "Jeff got it for me."

"Jeff? Who's Jeff?"

"Oh. My fiancé."

"Wait wait wait—your fiancé? You're engaged?"

She holds up her hand. There it is: a diamond on a platinum band. How'd he miss that? "Uh huh."

"You've been holding out on me! Hey—congratulations." They hug. "So when's the wedding?"

"In the fall."

Billy keeps smiling, really wide. "Well, that's great. That's great to hear. You're getting married! Wow, wow." His lips invert. "Hey, if I was out of line earlier..."

Michelle holds out her hand again—this time, palm forward. He could still see the band. "Forget about it. That was the past, remember?"

"Yeah. The past. So is—ah—Jeff here?"

Michelle presses her lips together and tilts her head to the side in an expression of polite sorrow. "He couldn't make it. He wanted to, but, well, he works for a consulting firm and he got called away to Mumbai for some product launch. He's—he's a really busy guy. And determined. Jeff spent probably about three months straight asking me out before I said yes."

"Really?"

"Yeah. We went to the same gym; that's how he noticed me. And he just had one date proposed after the next. It would be the Met by the free weights, a harbor cruise in the yoga room, a picnic in Central Park by the sauna. Finally, he got on his knees and begged me, pretty please, to tell him what it would take for me to go on a date—just one date—with him. I said, fine: McDonald's and a midnight movie."

"And that was that?"

"And that was that. He always gets what he wants, and he wants a lot. It's work work work work, and then it's squash and sky-diving and boat-racing. He's even an investor in a NASCAR team." The words pour on in a heavy list, made weightier, it seems, by habit.

"And he has you!"

"Well, he fits me into his schedule somehow."

"Somehow?"

Michelle smiles past that question. "So what about you? Where's your girlfriend tonight?"

"My girlfriend?" Billy looks around. "Well, I don't have one, right now."

"Really?"

"I guess I haven't found the right girl, the one who can put up with pork rinds and game tapes—or something."

"I guess it isn't the right time."

"Yeah. Time." He lingers on that word for a moment. "It can be really funny, I guess. I mean, I never would have thought ten years ago that I'd be here with you like this."

"We were pretty crazy back then."

"Yeah."

She smiles. "Remember that time on Halloween when a bunch of us broke into the cafeteria and had a dance?"

"Yeah," Billy says, laughing, "the Monster Mash. You were a princess."

"And you were a pirate. And then the police came and we all started to run. Somehow, you were with me, and you grabbed my hand. And we ran through the football fields and the forest until we were safe."

"It was so dark."

"You held my hand so tight, and you pulled me deeper and deeper into the night. Do you remember how we laughed, when we ran: almost like little joyful coughs because we didn't have breath for any more?"

"I do."

"We ran so fast, but you didn't let go."

"I didn't want to lose you."

"I think about that night sometimes." Her voice is soft and clear.

"So do I," Billy says. There's a momentary pause—like the pause of hanging fruit—before Billy picks up again with a smile. "You know, Adler called me into his office a few days after that. I almost think he thought *I* had something to do with that."

"The audacity—you only brought the decorations."

Billy nods. "I know, I know. But the thing is, in between all his lecturing about 'customary modes of respect' or whatever, I almost thought that he maybe approved, just a little, like our mischief was okay, like our fun wasn't all bad. Maybe."

"Maybe."

"He's still here, you know."

"Really?"

"Yeah, I was just talking to him. He looks the same as always. Some things, I guess, don't change."

"No, I guess some things don't."

The quiet returns. Billy puts his hands in his pockets. He waits a moment, feels the mantle of silence around them. It's thick, and it seems to buzz a little. There she is, there she is. And maybe there could be something, glorious and wonderful.

"It's really nice to see you, Michelle."

"It was great to see you, too, Billy."

"Say hi to Jeff for me."

"Ah—Jeff. I will."

"Tell him I'm glad—he's a lucky guy."

"Oh." She hugs him good-bye. "It was so good to see you. It really was."

"Yeah—very good."

"Yeah."

"Yeah."

Michelle starts to walk away. Billy watches her go—watches her stop and turn around and come back. "Billy?" she asks.

"Yeah?"

"Back then, if you had asked me out, I would have said yes."

Michelle turns and leaves him, stepping into the crowd.

Billy is alone.

The Tie That Binds

"Thank heavens for Medicare," Jim White said. "Without it, I'd still have glaucoma."

Jim's blustery voice had shot out over the little mumbling conversation, making everything else silent. Marcia, his wife, tightened her lips—there was her husband again, always making a scene. She glared at him. When he looked up from his conversation with Al Davis, Jim widened his eyes like he was giving an innocent, even confused, shrug. But he didn't say any more. It was supposed to be grand and auspicious, and his comment seemed, somehow, dirty.

So they all stood there in silence for a few minutes in that chill spring morning. Dorothy Hughes picked at her gray hair. Leonard Frank looked at his scuffed brown shoes. Rhonda Davis was trying to schedule in her head things to do while her grandchildren visited in a couple weeks; Al Davis was thinking about the basketball game of the night before, savoring the image of the three-pointer that won the game for the Celtics.

There were about fifteen of them in sum, all that was left of the congregation of the First Church of Middleboro, Vermont. Even a year ago, there had been more, but, with the decision to convert the church into a commemorative museum, the numbers had dwindled down to that dozen or so. And today was the last day. The final Sunday. Most of the men had coats and ties on.

The white church door in front of them creaked,
then opened. For the last time, the minister, Reverend
George A. Douglas, opened the door for the congregation. His once-rounded face had thinned in that nar-
rowed display of vigor in the aged. His white hair, still
full after all these years, swept across his head and
curled a little at its nicely-coifed edges. He was smiling
today as he opened the door, a smile of warm courage.

He led them forward. They entered, carrying battery-
powered electric candles, into the dark church. The
organ was silent; Ellie Shue marched with them. They
sang, that small chorus's voice rising in the shadows.

> *Blest be the tie that binds*
> *Our hearts in Christian love;*
> *The fellowship of kindred minds*
> *Is like to that above.*

Later, after the service, there was much handshak-
ing and hugging and even a few tears.

"Two hundred and three years," Dorothy Hughes
said as she hugged Reverend Douglas, "two centuries."

"I know," the minister said, nodding his head, "I
know. It's a lot of history."

"So much, so much," Marge Howard exclaimed as
she nodded her head even more vigorously, as though
each nod were another weight of insistence. "What with
Daniel Webster and *Ralph Waldo Emerson* and *Theo-
dore Parker* speaking here."

"We're very lucky to have that," Dorothy said.

"And that's why it's good that we'll be preserving this
history, for the public and for the future." The minister
had been one of the biggest advocates for, as he put it,
the "reform" of the church. "Change it to save it," he
had said, "to continue, to renew, its purpose."

Ellie Shue wasn't crying much, but she did wipe a
few tears from her face now and then with an ochre

handkerchief. "I was baptized in this church," she said to Melvin Whitlowe.

Melvin nodded. "I remember having my children baptized here." His voice, weakened with age, now almost sounded like an echoing yawn.

Ellie thought of her own children's births, and Stan's funeral service at First Church, now seven years gone by. "Oh, oh," she said quietly, more to herself than anyone else, "oh, oh."

After half the Swedish meatballs had been eaten and Mrs. Rattle's banana cream pie was only crumbs, the little party in the church basement entered that conversational Cold War, in which no one wants to be the first person to leave.

"Well," Rhonda said at last, a trifle loudly, "I have to get my hair done."

With a somber, almost mournful, kind of relief, the assembly began to dissipate.

"You woulda thought more woulda come than this," Jim said as he and his wife walked to the car.

Marcia hissed him to be quiet. "Not now."

"You know," Abner Schultz said (he must have overheard them), "some folks have gone over to Charity Chapel. You know, the one with the great bakesale?"

Marcia nodded. She had gone there a few years ago with a couple girlfriends and had gotten a very good bundt cake out of it; Jim and she had eaten half and then frozen the rest to save it.

"They're very welcoming there. I think—well I thought I might go."

Marcia looked up at her husband, who shrugged. "We'll have to think about that," she said to Abner.

Monday morning. Reverend Douglas was there, in jeans and a plaid shirt, along with a few others (Leonard had even gotten his daughter-in-law to help with the moving of things). "Good morning, Reverend Douglas," Ellie said as she walked up the lawn in the morning sun.

He laughed a little. "I'm not minister of much anymore. It's George—it's George." Most had called him by his first name for years now, anyways.

So *George* and the others began the slow process of cleansing and conversion. Much had to be removed—some of it donated, some of it sold, some of it thrown out. Though George had begun the titanic enterprise of sorting out paperwork to change the church to a museum, he still had to meet with the lawyer (graciously donating his time *pro bono*) in the morning or afternoon. Some of the back rooms, especially in the basement, had to undergo a thorough purgation. More than one mouse nest was found. Dust, some of it probably decades old, had to be swept from corners. The west stairs needed to be repaired—they had been blocked off for almost a decade due to a couple broken steps—so Cal Hartley and Melvin Whitlow went to work on those. Along with George Douglas, a few of the women (including Rhonda Davis, Marge Howard, and Dorothy Hughes) took on leading roles.

In addition to the physical transformations, there were also questions of intellectual ordering. First Church (or the former First Church) did indeed have prodigious stores of *history*; what to show? There were meeting on Tuesday and Thursday nights to discuss that very point, and the deliberations could stretch from six in the evening to eight-thirty or later. First, there were general discussions. A few points were settled even before any debate took place: the vestry was to become a library, the basement was to become an archive and holding area and place for administration, the cross, the one hewn by John Cotter at the very birth of the church, was to be put under glass by the door. But what else?

"I want a broad spectrum," George said at the outset. He was, in a way, the chair of the meetings.

So the debates began. Pamphlets from the visits of famous figures were pulled out of the archives. Rhonda Davis had an old dress from the late 1800s in a chest. They went about finding a mannequin for that. "A touch of history," Marge had chortled at the sight of its yellowed, tattered fabric. Old photographs were found. Deeds and plans—for the church, for town hall, for the old movie theater downtown—were dug up. A spittoon that Ulysses Grant had used was held up and debated. That, too, went in.

"This will be a place for the community," George announced at one meeting. "To record—to record and to remember." A sprinkle of applause burst out from the six-person assembly at that remark.

One night, as deliberations were nearing an end, Dorothy stood up and put a blue-veined hand to her chest. "I think you should all know that we are working on a place for history here. For history. For history." That firm declaration earned more sober, yet vigilant, nods.

So the reformation of the church (as a few called it with tiny smiles) went on. The old sign, the black letters of First Church, trimmed with a rainbow bar, was taken down. In its place: *The First Church of Middleboro Commemorative Museum.*

Marge was at first skeptical of the new name. "I think it should have been *The Commemorative Museum at the First Church.*"

But the others had won out. "After all," Rhonda said, "we want to make clear what this is. It has more flavor to it, this way."

"What about the organ?" Abner asked one afternoon as they were cleaning.

"We shall keep the organ," George said. "It was the first one in town, from what I can tell. It's a fine representative of the White Mountain school."

The museum would not, however, have sufficient funds to maintain the organ, not starting out at first, and its blower was already in troubled condition. So they disabled the blower. The great pipes, shining as the sun's light touched them, reaching to the ceiling, fell silent.

Marge, ever resourceful, soon suggested a new purpose for the organ. "You know, up there and everything, it would be great for photo-ops: take a picture of the kids, or something like that." It was an impressive sight, a few of the women agreed, nodding their heads.

The weeks went on. One Sunday, Marcia and Jim White went to Charity Chapel with Abner Schultz. Marcia saw Peggy James and Sue Highgrow there. They had organized the summer bazaar at First Church together. Marcia smiled to see them and all the other welcoming faces. When Peggy leaned over to invite her to the Women's Club brunch after the service ("You know, to catch up."), Marcia smiled and happily accepted. They had such a good time laughing over pancakes that Marcia knew she had to come back the next Sunday. Jim shruggingly accepted his wife's interest, so the couple began its regular attendance at Charity Chapel. Soon, in between afternoon teas and rummage sales and those Sunday brunches, Marcia felt quite at home at the new church. Only in certain moments did she feel a pang—was it loss?—for the days at First Church and how it had been. Once, she mentioned that loss to Peggy and Sue, and the three aged ladies had bent their lips and bobbed their heads in a weighty, but comfortable, expression of grief. "Well, those things happen," Sue had said. The other two had nodded at this wisdom.

A new coat of paint—a crisp green—was put on the front door. That Friday, the members of this reforming band were readying themselves for the upcoming weekend. The display cases were due to arrive, and the pews had to be removed. "That's going to be a hard thing," Al had said, looking at the solid wooden seats.

"That's why Jack and the boys have to help us," Rhonda said.

Al nodded. "They'll be there. They'll be there." Their son was coming to help with the U-Haul. They were donating them, but the pews still had to make it to the outskirts of Boston. With the help of children and grandchildren, they pushed on with the sweaty work of removing the pews. Jack Davis didn't look too excited to be driving the giant truck filled with that clanking wood, but, with a wave, he drove away.

Marge was smiling broadly on Monday morning. "Well, I say. It's beginning to look like a *proper* museum."

All the old pews had been pulled away, aside from one put on display at the side. The cases were there, with some of the pamphlets and other artifacts stored within them. "It's the best kind of glass," Dorothy said (for the case selection was her purview). "It protects against the sun. The bases are acid-free. This stuff should be preserved for a long, long time. Free from corruption. I think that's their motto. It was worth paying a little more—for value like that."

The work on the transformation of the vestry into a library, the deep joy of George's heart, was also coming apace. "It's a perfect size for it," he would say when bringing up the plan. The walls were lined with shelves. George would sometimes look up at the high wall at one end, stacked with books, and a thin smile would reach across his lined face. The thought of scholars coming and settling down with pencils and notebooks and perusing the various books—it all seemed very important to him and almost (though he couldn't quite admit it to himself) somewhat mystical, like Halloween, maybe, to a young child.

They were all there, the books acquired by ministers throughout the years of First Church as well as the various nineteenth-century (he had an affinity for that time) volumes George himself had acquired. A few members of the congregation had even donated some aged books. The great names were there, so much history. Mather (Increase and Cotton). Edwards's sermons. Beecher (Lyman and Henry Ward). Charles Grandison Finney. Emerson. Parker. Renan (an early American edition of the *Vie de Jésus*!). William James. Niebuhr. He still remembered dwelling with "old Reinhold," as he called him, in his days training for the ministry. The words were hard, fast, and heavy. Those were his old copies up there. Sometimes, there would be a twinge of sadness, followed by a shrug. Well, he had put those things aside. There were newer names, too, ones that told the story of the past few decades. Tillich. Altizer.

Of course, there were books not only on theology, nor books solely from a Christian perspective. No, this library would present, as he thought to himself, a "rainbow of social justice." It would memorialize the efforts of people striving for a better world in this world.

One afternoon, as George was leafing through the brittle yellow pages of one of the congregation registers, Marge entered. "So you like the looks of things in here, George?"

He looked up, allowing his finger to rest on the margin of a page. It had that nice smoothness to it, the one old books could sometimes have. "It's going very well, Marge. This is like the heart of it, I think, in some ways."

"Well, I can see that. You certainly spend a lot of time in here."

"Yes," he said softly, putting the book back on the shelf with a slow reverence, "yes."

Marge asked, "You really believe in this, don't you?"

"I do," he said, nodding, "yes I do. It's an important project." It was just them in the building, and, with Marge lingering at the door, George could almost feel like he was talking to himself. "You face so many things, so many questions. That troubled me for a long time. But then, I realized that I'd never find the answers to those questions. So I put them by." He shrugged. "And here we are. And this we *know*"—he lifted one of the old books lying on the table—"is right here."

When she was forty-two, Ellie Shue began to notice a stiffness in her wrists. Then, a slight swelling. She started to feel it in her fingers, too. The doctors told her it was arthritis. They tried medications. Some worked better than others, but none erased the pain. The years accumulated, and the range of motion diminished. Her finger joints swelled into knobs, and her hands, with time, began to resemble claws.

Ellie loved music. Stan would tut her: "It's lucky I got to you before the piano did." But he always said that in the warm way he had, and his voice was always smiling. It made her smile when he said that—especially later, when they were all alone in the old house on Canterbury Lane. "Play the piano for me, Ellie," he'd say, and she would. She would have played it anyways, even if he hadn't asked, but Stan knew she liked a willing audience.

The piano and organ were where the arthritis could hurt the most. But she didn't let the pain win. She kept playing at church and for herself and Stan and whoever else would listen. Sometimes, there were moments when the pain would sink beneath the rush of music. Sometimes, it would be there still and fuse with the sound, like rocks with waves crashing over them. Yes, the rocks were there—but the water was, too.

Reverend Douglas had tried to convince her to give up her music duties. "But who else would do it?" she had asked. He could never answer that. Yes, some other members did play the piano, but no one else wanted to at church, not for everyone. The minister had said they could just have pre-recorded music. Even then, even in her seventies, Ellie had drawn herself up and said, "I can do it still."

The minister wasn't one to quarrel over these matters, but he did refer to them once or twice. One day, just a year or so before, he might have been exasperated and said (rather intemperately, she thought), "Give it up, Ellie. Is it really worth the pain?"

"I can bear it," she had said, very firmly. "I can bear it." Reverend Douglas had smiled in that way he had when he thought he had been defeated—his lips smushed together as though they would crush any further word of remonstrance in their wry twist. Other than sometimes lingering with his eyes (watching Ellie go to practice, looking at the song numbers on the placard at the front of the church, gazing at the assorted salves by the organ), he didn't make any more mention of the topic.

The minister went to visit her one day. "Ellie," he said.

"Reverend Douglas."

"It's—" he began but then stopped himself. "So. How've you been?"

"Oh, I've been alright."

"Haven't really seen you at the, ah, museum."

She held up her bent hands. "These aren't the best for moving things like that." She started to laugh. He laughed, too, in tight little chuckles.

"Well, it would be good to see you there. Even if you didn't want to do anything, just to watch. You used to spend a lot of time there."

"I did." She didn't ask about the organ.

There was that awkward silence, the one that could happen between them sometimes. "Have you found a new church, Ellie?" He knew that would be a concern of hers.

"Jim and Marcia White have taken me to Charity Chapel a few times. It's very generous of them."

"I hear it's a nice church."

"They're very welcoming to me, and they have a nice organ."

"Have you been able to play it yet?" he asked.

Shaking her head, Ellie pressed her wrinkled pale lips together in an almost-smile. "Not yet, not yet."

With any reform, the final touches can be the hardest part. There were debates about where to put a given case, what to use a certain shelf for, how much to charge (three dollars? five?), and so many details. Little spots were always found that needed more cleaning. Dorothy felt like she spent a week walking around the museum with a bottle of Windex in hand. Melvin kept sweeping, his pale skin standing out against the chipped black paint of the broom handle. It seemed as though more dust was always being kicked up. Marge kept finding things that needed to be done. "Details, details," she would declare.

And then, somehow, it was done. One morning, the three or four workers realized how little there was left. The inside had been transformed; it looked, as Dorothy said, *presentable*. So many things were gone; those that stayed were thoroughly rearranged. So much new was here! "This is it," Rhonda said, "this is it."

So one Friday in July at 5:00, balloons floated from the sign at the front of *The First Church of Middleboro Commemorative Museum*. Inside, stretching from the old choir loft, multicolored streamers hung. Tables were set up, laden with sparkling cider bottles and crackers and little squares of cheese overlapping like fish scales. The tinkling notes of the Middleboro Jazz Trio played underneath the muted conversation of the festive assembly. Many of the town councilors were there, and a lot of the old members of First Church had come by. They were almost universally admiring.

"Look at that!"

"A-maz-ing!"

"I just don't know how you did it."

In her floral-print dress, Marge rushed from one convivial knot to the next. Her laughter rose above the mumbling din like a rearing horse. Her high-kicking words flew up in spurts. "You gotta see this...and she was here day and night...you must know...of course of course...that's awful...I don't know how..." She seemed almost glowing with attention or with pleasure. When she sensed a quieting of the crowd's discussion, she went toward the pulpit. Others noticed, and the noise shrank with her steps.

"Well everyone," she said loudly, "thank you all for coming to the grand opening of *The First Church of Middleboro Commemorative Museum*." She joined in with the applause that sprouted up. "Now a lot of people put a lot of work into this, but I think we should hear from someone who's been a driving force in this from the beginning. Someone who has helped guide this church back when it was still a church, a dear friend of mine. He's always got something interesting to say. *George Douglas!*" She indicated him with a wave. *Clap clap clap clap* as the crowd focused on him.

"Oh," he said, holding a wine glass in his hand as he turned from conversation with a councilor.

"Come on, George," Marge responded.

"Come on, George, just a few words," Rhonda cried.

"Speech speech," Abner began, and the crowd took it up: *Speech speech speech speech speech speech.*

Smiling a little and nodding his head, George accepted. "Alright, alright." Clapping of pleasure.

"Up in the pulpit," Al Davis called out, "for old times' sake." There was some laughter and harder applause.

George held up a hand to ward off that request. "No, no, no," he said quietly. "I think I'll stay right here."

The crowd began to bumble a little as it waited.

George spoke. "I knew when we started there were some doubters. *It can't be done.* Or, *It's too hard.* Or, *It'll take too long.* But I had faith that, if we buckled down, were consistent, and just kept at it, we'd get there. And now, with a little—with a lot of—elbow grease, it doesn't look too bad, I think." A burst of applause; a few men whistled.

George tilted his head in a reflective pose and waited a moment before continuing. Then, as he always could, he launched out upon the silence of the assembled. "You know, what we're doing here isn't just about us. It's about something bigger. It's about our commitment to history, to the community, to those around us and after us and, yes, before us. We should record their struggle. We should give testimony of their efforts. I know some of us are what some people might call in late middle age—maybe even *old.*" There were a few bubbling chuckles. "But the old matters. And we can always keep it new in our efforts. We can keep faith with the past. And we can contribute to that ever-evolving human story: the trials, hopes, fears, hurts, and joys of men and women throughout the ages. Today, we have begun part of that preservation of the stories of generations, and we can begin to spread those stories—to share them—with our own community and with the broader world. Their stories do not end, for their stories blend into our own.

"Our actions testify to our belief in this. We have brought forward their stories. And Marge and Rhonda and Dorothy and Melvin and all the other folks who have helped—thank you. In fact, let's have everyone give them a hand." The hand is duly given: an eddy of clapping.

"We couldn't have done it without all that effort," George continued. "We believed this could be done. We believed it was worth doing. And look at where our belief has gotten us." The sweep of his open hand ran across the display cases and refreshments and books and disabled organ and cash register and handouts for tourists and all the framed images and the crowd brought together by the cause. The cheers and applause rose in a sustained gush.

Far away from the crowd chatting into the final pinky-yellow hues of the dusk, Ellie Shue sat hunched over her piano in her worn house on Canterbury Lane. An old hymnal, which she had rescued from the ones going to the dump, was perched on top of the piano. The pain simmered a little as she played. The notes and chords rang through the tired, time-bitten wood of the piano. The yellowed keys, pressed by gnarled fingers, still set the hammers to singing.

She played, the knots of pain in her fingers, her wrists, her shoulders swelling with every note. Her voice was like shuffling sandpaper.

"Hallelujah...Hallelujah...Hal-le-lu-u-jah..."

An Aria of Windrows

Hey, sorry I missed you. Catch you later.

I play that message again and again and again. It sustains me, with its haunting contingencies, throughout the day.

Hey, sorry I missed you. Catch you later.

It is a feminine voice. Youngish. The voice is untarnished, curling, cute, the way that young women can be cute.

Its contingencies. A whole web of existence—of habits, passions, coincidences, essences—held that phrase; a silver strand of it had drifted into my life.

Wrong number. *Catch you later.*

At the office: *Hey, sorry I missed you. Catch you later.* The phone held up to my ear, like it was some business call, some important contact. *Hey, sorry I missed you. Catch you later.*

Like a dream, like the distant notes of a carousel, the silver curls.

Is this my face, I ask myself. Is this my leonine face. The jaw, jutting. Eyes hooded by bone.

What is it like—to live your whole life like you're just waiting for each day to end? I live that way. That was the end—the end. Just the setting of the sun. A kind of teleology of despair.

The sun's light runs out.

In the morning, the dulling enchantment of habit is least. I usually don't eat in the morning, finding no pleasure in food.

It is amazing how much passion is spent for something that is over so quickly.

I long ago lost all squeamishness about food. Beetles, raw sealife, herbs—only a second, and it is done. You can numb yourself to the mouth. You realize it only as substance. Carrion flavors, decayed tastes. There is only the crunching.

Teeth rending the day.

How much goes into making something. Each potato chip's a grand symphony of life. How much has woven together to get that potato chip to your hand. One might say it's the work of a universe's lifetime. The dirt, the nutrients, the seeding, the generations of men behind that one hand that operates the combine...the hand that sticks itself into the plastic glove at the factory...the hand at the factory for the plastic glove...behind the delivery truck...the wheels forging hot...so much, so much...the list's as long as it is hackneyed. Everything's like that.

Everything's a symphony.

The grandest symphony is but a tinning note.

It withers, with time, in time, as time...

Everything's the same like that...

No wonder we're deaf.

Hey, sorry I missed you. Catch you later.

Himmaleh—I can only bear so much...

So much bearing becomes a weightlessness.

But the hours are so heavy.

The shower runs like sunlight down my body, like lit tears, drops of lead.

There is no lightness in the dawn, now.

We humans are mimics. Maybe that's how advertising saves us. It tells us to care, like art does. We see men caring, or seeming to care. We can't tell the difference. Mimicry delivers us, fools us, our fooling our deliverance.

Waiting—waiting stretches time. The emptiness crowds the space around us. When you're waiting for something—that's when you know how long the time takes. If you're busy, time flies, like buzzing insects. You're so distracted by the thousand things that you gain the illusion of immersive purposiveness.

But when there's nothing...that's what time is: the awareness of nothingness. You're waiting at the gas station for the moment when the pump initializes—after you've swiped your credit card, the gas tank's open, and there's only the waiting. It seems to take so long. You wonder if the gas will ever start to flow. Maybe it won't.

Do I contradict myself? Well, I guess I do. I stopped trying to order my multitudes.

There is only the flashing.

I think about her, making that call. Perhaps in her bedroom, just after checking her lipstick in the novelty-framed mirror. Or on the street, while waiting for the light to change. Or on the street, walking with the sun in her hair. Or on some field, as a thought crosses her mind that she should dial my number. Or in a hallway at a bar, as the cocktails roil in her skull. Or while having coffee—or tea—with a friend. Or while she's at work, bored. Or she's in front of the TV. Or waiting in line at some government office. There had been some opening in her life, as the doors slid open, as she made that call.

Had her heart skipped as a stone across the trembling waters? A deliberate pouncing? I have listened again and again to that message. Every time is a trial of the timbre of her voice. I can peel apart reverberation after reverberation. I hold it in my memory, rotate it around like the diagram of some building. I hazard one guess, then another. Then I listen to it again. Sometimes, I am shocked to notice how different it is from all my memories. I am rarely disappointed, as I am by so much else, by the poverty of that renewed experience.

Hey, sorry I missed you. Catch you later.

How many thoughts can attend me there, on the phrase? You would think there tedium would at last deliver me. The words would be hollow, hackneyed. They would be like sheets flapping in the wind—noise, as everything else becomes noise. Could I get numb to that, as everything else?

It remains fresh air in the locked box of my mind. We all have our chinks. Perhaps that is mine.

My thoughts march up and down. *Hey, sorry I missed you. Catch you later.* Always, always that rhythm.

I have spent whole days thinking about it, not knowing that I was thinking about it. I would walk in the park, go grocery shopping, slump in a bar stool and drink out my brains with three people I call my friends. And there would be this little burr animating my brain. I wouldn't know it. Then, suddenly, after the seventh beer, through the haze, the phrase would come back. In the middle of a football game—*Hey, sorry I missed you. Catch you later.* Staring out the window after four hours of watching post-midnight TV—*Hey, sorry I missed you. Catch you later.*

Was it a mistake—that I was not there to answer the phone? Some unfortunate cosmic coincidence? Some galactic confusion? Had I done something wrong?

Could I be responsible—for that? At a certain point, ignorance of ill intention does only so much to assuage a sense of guilt or grief.

Bureaucrats aspire to trap us in a cage, but, in doing so, they merely show us how much fun dullness can be. Many websites—most of the interesting ones—are blocked at work. But web search engines are not. Sometimes, I will type in a phrase ("elephant shoes," for example, or "blob" or "catch you later") and scroll through the results. Page by page. The first page of results...the tenth...the hundredth. The fragmentary few sentences below the website heading are enough. I can make do with fragments. It's amazing how an afternoon can go by like that. It's amazing how strong habit is—how I will do this at home, too, even though there's no need.

But that's the thing—you realize that burr has been whirling around in your brain. That's why I was unhappy. That's why I've been washing my car and vacuuming it out. That's why I've been on the phone for hours talking with people, some of whom I haven't spoken to for months. That's why I'm reviewing my bills like this or scanning software or something.

It's that voice. That feeling. Those intensities of phantasms.

Despair need not be an elevating feeling. It need not bring you down into the deepest abyss. The plains of despair are perhaps the worst of all—a desert, flat as far as the eye can see. You might even weep at the cactus. With joy or sorrow—it would be something.

It is easy for flesh to bleed. But for the heart...but for the heart...

I can make do with fragments. Some fragments are like threads that weave. You see them only by parts—but there is a whole.

Well, we all have our hopes.

Even if those hopes are measured out by coffee spoons. Who was it? Could I have known her? If we had spoken—might there have been something? Ah, *something*. When did that become an opportunity for joy? There's something intoxicating about *something*, like there could be something different.

Hey, sorry I missed you. Catch you later.

No one around me knows of this message. No one knows of the secret that little cell phone carries—that I carry. It is like an act of resistance against my everyday not to tell them. It is perhaps one of the last acts I am capable of in that it is not really a resistance. It is a standing aside. It would be nothing to them, perhaps.

I wonder sometimes, if they do not have their own secret artifacts, or relics. We coast along, ignorant of those private passions, if passions they can be called. We would never understand each other, perhaps. *Hey, sorry I missed you. Catch you later.* Would they understand? That thought lingers on my lips and makes me want to turn to the person in the cubicle next to me or standing behind me in line at the pharmacy. Would you want to listen? With a smile, I would ask, like inviting them into a brave new world. List, oh list.

But I never do. What difference would it make?

I would still be in my own shoes.

The end of the day comes, as it always does. The sun's light withers. I know my body is tiring. I know my mind is tired. That tiredness has been my constant companion for more than those sixteen hours. The moon rises, or it doesn't. The clouds form, or they don't. The raindrops fall, or snowflakes, or nothing. The night is here. And after that night another day, another night. The earth goes on, unthinking.

Then, in the blue thoughts and empty rituals...then, in the turning back the sheets....then, as the thoughts run aground, as they always do...sleep will bring me no relief. There is just the quiet mockery of desolation. No relief—no no no.

There is death, and there is the putting off of death.

But this?

I have not seen the sun turn, not for so long.

Hey, sorry I missed you. Catch you later.

The Other Side

(A manuscript by Alyssa Gartner)

Doctor Snydecker, since you wanted me to keep a log of my experiences, here it is. I'm probably going to do it wrong but I'll try anyways.

The way I currently am right now—it's like trying to ride a bicycle. I just have to keep my balance. And it can be really tricky. Sometimes I think I'm just about to fall over or tumble into a ditch. I was used to walking, and now it's like I'm in someplace completely different.

I don't know why I'm telling you all this. Maybe it's because I don't have anyone else to tell. It's awfully lonely, Doctor, awfully lonely being me right now. I love my husband. I really do. You have to believe that. It's just—it's just that things are different, now. Maybe it was all my headaches before. Maybe they started it. It's not that Mark was never willing to care for me. He was. The first night I woke up crying so bad with the headache, he got me Advil and hot cloths and everything. He held me the whole night, even though he had to get up for work early the next day. And he never worried about doctors and he was always there to take me to any appointments, especially when I couldn't drive on my own. But maybe it's just that all the pain added up. Maybe that was it. Maybe it became like a wall or sponge or something and it sucked up all the air.

Maybe it was all the extra time Mark had to work to pay for the medical bills. I see how much he has to work, and it's hard work.

Maybe it's because of the secrets. Maybe I just got used to trying to hide my headaches and then those strange things from him, so I didn't mind hiding everything else.

You were right, by the way. Practice helps. Now my head doesn't even hurt from writing, not too much. But it hurts a little now, so I think I'll stop.

June 8
Okay. You wanted the story, the whole account, you said or something like that. Well, here it goes.

So it started with the headaches. I don't mean headaches like a belt a little too tight around your skull—I'm talking about headaches that seem like a flaming chain's going to pop your head like a zit or like some big iron spike right through your brain. They came out of nowhere just after I turned 23.

No one really knew what caused them, and nothing really helped. When I had one of them, I'd just have to lie down in the darkness—no lights, no sounds, no nothing. You get a weird sense of privacy like that. Sometimes, especially earlier, Mark would be there with me in the darkness, and I'd just listen to his breathing and mine, and maybe I'd feel a little bit better.

The doctors gave me brain scans. Nothing. Blood tests didn't show anything. It's like there was some mystery in my body, one that those men in white coats couldn't understand.

After a while, I had to stop working. I liked my job enough. I worked at the make-up counter at Macy's. It was fun in its own way—judging which blush would be best for someone's skin color, say, or showing them the best way to apply foundation. I had a good time, and the girls I worked with were pretty nice.

But then the headaches started to get worse. They made me unreliable. If I was going to be knocked out by a headache, the manager couldn't depend on me to work a counter alone. Things got harder on my nerves, too. Sometimes, a counter display would get knocked over. People around me blamed mall rats. I did, too.

Sometimes the pain would get so bad that I'd just lie on the floor's white tiles, curled up in a ball. My last day was my worst day. I should have known it would be a really bad one. As soon as I woke up, it seemed like some screw was turning in my head. But I went to work (I didn't want to call in sick again), and it soon got really bad.

Even when I closed my eyes, the light through my eyelids was a white-hot rake. I covered my face, said I needed to go to the bathroom. It felt like I had molten lava climbing up my throat. I don't remember walking to the bathroom. I do remember some flood of relief as I opened the door and saw the tiny brown tiling. I thought, for a moment, I might put some water on my face. Maybe that would help. But then all I remember is blackness.

When I woke up, my face was against the tile. Something smelled. I looked around and saw vomit streaked across the door of a stall, dribbling down the front of the toilet, smeared along the floor. My eyes were kinda weird when I was waking up, because it almost looked neon—like some fluorescent green-yellow knot of rivers all around me. I sat up. Some was on me, too. I tried to wash it off with a few splashes of water. My head didn't hurt as much, I realized, even if I did look miserable.

When I came back, I saw that a mannequin had fallen right through part of my station. Had I pulled it down in running? I couldn't remember.

My supervisor brought me into the backroom. She was really gentle. She sat me down, asked me how I was, said I didn't look so good. "Hon," she said, "maybe you should rest up for a while until you get better before coming back to work."

"I'm sorry," I said. I was crying, then. Not just about the mannequin—about everything.

"It's okay," she said. "It's okay." She kept repeating that as she patted me on the back and walked me out of the store.

She was really nice like that. She made it seem like it wasn't my fault, like she really cared. That made me even sadder.

June 9

The more time I spent around the house, the weirder things seemed. Maybe it's like that—when you spend most of the day alone, since you're not distracted, maybe you start to see strange things. At first, it was little things, things I had noticed even while I was working. Things like a misplaced pair of earrings or something. Things falling down—like a toilet brush or my lipstick on the dresser—things that anything could have caused. Or maybe my closet would be open when I could have sworn that it was closed. I never told Mark about those things. I didn't even know for sure that *things* were happening, and I didn't need him to worry about me even more.

I didn't know if Mark saw anything, then. They were really easy to miss, at first. I'm sure I missed a lot— didn't see how that one thing was just a little different. Sometimes, I had this floating feeling of strangeness.

And then it started to get worse. You almost think you can get used to it, you even try to pretend it's normal, but it isn't, and you know it.

To give you an idea of what it was like, here's what happened on the day when things really started to change, the day that set me on the path to getting your book out of the library.

It was breakfast. I found out that one of the ways of coping with my headaches was to speak under my breath, to give my mind something to focus on and distract me from the pain. So I was saying something.

"What?" Mark asked.

"What?"

"What did you say?"

"Me?" Had he heard that?

"You just said something?"

What had I said? I couldn't remember. Maybe it was about the frozen waffles. I couldn't remember those things, sometimes. The words were just place holders, and they would just flow. Like a river. I put my hand to my head, trying. I was really trying.

"What is it?" Some of the snap had drained out of his voice. Concern replaced it.

"Nothing—just my, just my..."

"It's your head."

I didn't want to admit it—right before he went off to work—but I didn't want to lie, not too much. "It's not too bad."

That got Mark all irritated, and he started to ask about Dr. Holmes and if he really hadn't given any hint about what went wrong. And then the irritation flipped. Mark could be funny like that. He'd get upset, and then get sorry.

"Sorry, sorry," he said as he got up to go to work. He saw my eyes maybe watering a little. I don't know why

they had done that after I said, "Things can change."
Maybe it was because of the pain.

I followed him to the living room, watched him shut
the door hard behind him. The sound exploded in my
head.

I hadn't bothered to mention that it was our two-
year anniversary. Neither had he.

When I walked back to the kitchen, all the cabinet
doors were swung open. So was the refrigerator door.
The oven was open, too.

With that pain in my head, I just couldn't face it.
Shutting the door of the fridge and the oven, I left
everything else where it was and went to bed. Sometimes, sleeping helped.

June 10
So I slept, but not for too long.

Crash.

My eyes flashed open. What was that?

Crash.

It seemed like something was holding me by the
throat. I lay in bed, waiting. What could it be? Had
anyone broken in? Maybe some kids had knocked a
baseball through the glass? I waited in the pounding
semi-darkness. I couldn't hear anything else. No
footsteps or anything. There was silence.

Quietly quietly quietly, I got out of bed. I picked up
one of Mark's sneakers (it seemed the best type of
weapon I could easily grab) and crept toward the door.
Quietly quietly quietly I opened the door. The hinges
didn't even have a trace of a squeal. Still no sounds.

"Mark?" I called. Maybe he had come home early.

Nothing.

I heard—a hawk scream outside.

My stomach was all curled up as I took the first step out of my bedroom. Nothing. No sign of movement. I padded around the house—living room, extra room (we didn't have a name for that yet), bathroom. Nothing. I walked into the kitchen, and the shoe dropped onto the floor.

The plates from breakfast lay shattered on the floor. I could see the point of impact: the syrup stain about shoulder-high on the wall. I looked down at the broken bits. I looked around at the empty room.

I wanted to throw up, and not because of any pain in my head.

That was the first time I felt really truly afraid in this house. I had been afraid before, and felt weird about faucets that I thought I had shut off still trickling on, or things falling down, or whatever, but it had never been like that. Never that fear reaching right down to my bones. It was at that moment, looking at those jagged dirty fragments on the floor, that I felt that my life was one-hundred-percent out-of-control.

I wondered if maybe things would start to get violent. What would be next—the knives?

I swept up the plate fragments, vacuumed where they fell, and didn't tell Mark. Maybe he'd think that I was lying. Maybe he'd think that I was going crazy. *What—a* ghost *did it?* I didn't know what else it could be. So I didn't say anything. I figured he wouldn't notice that the plates were missing. So I kept that shattering, like so much else, my secret.

June 11
It's kinda emotional to write all this stuff out, you know. It brings it all back. Mark was tired when he came home from work today. It's like he's thinking

about something. He didn't say too much at all during dinner or after. He doesn't have to work tonight, but he went out anyways. I don't know where. I don't really ask anymore.

So anyways, I started to look things up. That was a slow process; after a few minutes of reading on the laptop, my head would start to pulse a little. I could manage it a little better when it was type on a page. So one afternoon, when I knew Mark would definitely be busy all day, I walked down a few streets and took the bus to the library. It was a little scary to ride the bus all alone like that (I kept hoping the pain wouldn't get too bad), but I stayed on it and got to the library. The library downtown has a great collection of books on the paranormal—did you know that? That's where I found *The Other Side*. I couldn't believe that, when I looked at the back cover, I saw that you—Dr. J. L. Snydecker—actually lived in the same town as me. That sealed the deal.

When I got home, I poked through the book, the sections on ghosts, haunted houses, and that sort of thing. I didn't look too much before Mark got home, but, the next day, I read more.

That's when I hit upon the sentence, the one that changed my whole view. I've got the book here (thanks again for giving me a copy), so I'll write it out: *Individuals who suspect that their house may be haunted could also be experiencing the effects of undiagnosed telekinetic powers*. I put the book down for a second and blinked. It was a hard blink, too, like my eyes were trying to fasten onto something solid, and the edges of my eyelids really did feel firm. Telekinesis?

My head was starting to be filled with fog (and pain and, yes, a little anxiety) as I flipped to the index. I found the section on telekinesis, and then I started to get cold. The "adult-onset" of telekinetic sensitivity, the "unconscious manifestation" in the early stages of telekinesis, in which "the subject may experience unexpectedly closing doors, flickering lights, and so forth," the "at times crippling headaches," all these things were just like me.

But even after I felt those chills, I put the book down and almost shook my head. Telekinesis? Me? Like I could just make that broom over there pop into my hands. I looked at the broom. I tried, somehow, to will it into my hands. Nope. Nothing. What about that magazine across the room? Why not? Will will will. Nothing nothing nothing.

Feeling kind of silly for all that willing, I went about some chores. I was feeling pretty good. Just a little bit of a headache, a few echoes around my temples. So I was walking around. And my hands made that broom sweep, and my hands stuck that magazine back with the others in the basket.

Putting some laundry into the closet in the bathroom, I was thirsty and got myself a little cup of water—one of those disposable ones. I drank a little, then the phone rang, so I put that cup down on the sink and went to answer it. Wrong number. I came back and started putting the towels away again. Telekinesis! Shaking my head as I reached up for the highest shelf, I was thirsty. If I had telekinesis, I could have wished that little cup right into my hand. Right there, just floating off—

I felt the splash of water first. Then I heard the paper cup hit the tiles, that little hollow *tdunk tdunk tdunk*.

June 12

Was I excited when I heard that sound? Well, I almost didn't believe it. But I figured I'd try.

So the next day, I just spent hours concentrating on that tiny little paper cup. I sat at the kitchen table and stared and stared and stared. Sometimes, veins of pain tightened in my head, cutting through the thickening fog of tiredness. But I didn't stop. I waited them out, and they passed, or at least weren't so bad. I forgot to eat. I didn't care about eating. I turned off all the lights. I turned the faucet on to full blast. I turned off the faucet.

I sat and closed my eyes and tried to picture the cup before me. I tried to fill in the void with all the little flowers and colors. I thought of its shape, the slight crease at its lip caused by me pulling it too quickly out of the dispenser. I thought of it just sitting there. It was there, in a certain point of space. I tried to think of its curve. I tried to feel the curves in my head. I tried—I know this sounds weird—to become the curves, to make them in my brain. I just kept running around and around those curves. A circle's like that: you can end right where you start and just keep going. It was like all those thin little curves were inching up the cup. Then they were all together. I thought of twisting those curves—just a little bit. They spun. They spun. They kept spinning.

Then there was a sound. It was like a gorilla falling into a swimming pool. I opened my eyes.

The cup was on the floor.

I sank back into the kitchen chair, and it felt like I was feeling the wood for the first time.

When Mark got back, he was covered in green paint. "So I was painting some trim, Julio's painting above me, and, then, somehow, he knocks the can over or something and spills this all over me. I got some of it off."

"Well, you go shower." I smiled. "Dinner's just about ready, honey."

I didn't tell him then, either. Maybe that was bad. But I wanted to be able to do it when I wanted to, at least before I showed him. I couldn't, then. I can't even always do it now.

Remember how I went to see you in your office, and I tried to move that mini dental floss, and I couldn't? But then suddenly it flew across the room? I didn't even mean it to that time, but it did. I don't really know my powers yet. I can barely get things to move now, sometimes. And sometimes—maybe you'll want to know this—it seems like there's a backlash effect or something. It's like a rubber band, maybe. You stretch it too far and it can slip out of your grip and snap back at you. I guess I have to learn to be patient, to give and to push at the right moments. Some days, it's like it bounces back, and my head hurts for hours. But I guess it's a good kind of hurt. It's the hurt that I'm doing something, something I really should be doing. It's nice to know that, and it makes a difference, I guess.

June 14

A day or so after what happened with the cup, there was kinda a close call.

Mark noticed the book. I was sitting watching TV, when he came up behind me.

"*The Other Side*. This your book?"

"Yeah, I got it at the library, since I was feeling a little bit better."

"What's it about—like ghosts and stuff like that?"

"Yeah." Okay—my throat was feeling a little tight there.

"You think this house is haunted or something?" He was smiling all funny like.

I shook my head in little twitches. "No. No. No." I didn't think it was, but I didn't know what to tell him. *Actually, honey, I think I might have telekinetic powers.* Yeah, that'd work.

He flipped over to the back and made a show of looking it over. "You believe in this stuff?"

I smiled. "I thought it would be funny to read it."

"Hmm," he said and dropped the book on the couch as he walked out of the room. To me, it felt like he was dropping an anvil.

I sat in front of the TV for a few more minutes, letting my chest unclench—but my chest tightened again when I heard his steps coming closer down the hallway again.

"If something was wrong, you'd tell me, right?"

I looked over my shoulder at him. "Why wouldn't I?" I tried to make my voice all smooth and airy. He didn't say any more.

June 16
It's weird how these things can come out of nowhere. It's...it's—I know you'll laugh, but it's like magic. I thought my life was one way and, then, suddenly it isn't. It's weird how people can have these abilities *latent* (I think that's the word you used), and they can just spring up in them—sometimes even without headaches (though you say headaches are by far one of the most common side effects of adult onset). I know you said something about the later stages of brain formation in the 20s or something, and maybe that's

just it. Just to wake up and have it—a new part of yourself, a part that was always there.

I sometimes wonder what Mark would say if I did tell him. Would he believe me at first? I almost think it would hurt a lot if he didn't believe me right there, if there was that moment of doubt. I could show him—I'd want to be able to show him—but I wonder if he would believe me without seeing, or before seeing.

Mark was a year ahead of me in high school. I saw him sometimes at parties. Our first date was his junior prom. He just went up to me in the hallway by my locker and asked me out. I asked him *why me?* And he just looked at me and said, "Who else would I ask?" He was smiling. Later, I found out that he had liked me for a while. It felt right when we danced and when we kissed.

He's got a great smile when he really smiles, like he used to, and he's got perfect teeth (I know you'd appreciate that, Doctor). Mark's so strong. You should see him painting. The way he just tosses up a ladder or scrambles up it. He did construction for a little bit. He could just lift that lumber so easily.

I had a headache for most of the day, so I thought about that.

June 17
I couldn't get anything to move today. I guess my brain's still adjusting. You said that could happen, right? (Though I guess you also said that I was the first case of "demonstrated telekinesis" that you had seen in person. What makes something demonstrated, I wonder?) You know earlier, when I talked about concentrating on the cup—I think that's how my power works. It's not like you'd think from a movie, when you just

think "I want that plate to move," and it moves. Or maybe it is like that, but only when you're more experienced. For me, right now, I have to think about things a certain way. Only then—if everything else's right—will they move. It's like learning how to read: first, you concentrate on one letter at a time and then you just glide over whole words. When I first learned what I could do, I went around trying everything in the house—to see what I could move, to test my powers (to test myself!) out. It was a lot of fun, just going through and trying. I couldn't get most things to move (of if they did move, they only shifted a little bit), but I felt free, like a kid running through some fancy dinner, tasting everything she can.

June 21
I spent a lot of time practicing today. I can't lift too much. It's like heavier things are harder to wrap my mind around. It's almost like there's more stuff to wrap or it takes more concentration or something. It takes time to learn how to move those things through space, too. You have to keep all the curves together, matching in the same position, so you have to get them all at once. That's why my first uses of the power were like smacks. *Whap*—and something goes flying. I'm getting better at keeping it together now. I can slide things across a table (then I don't need to worry about the curves in the same way). Moving things in the air is harder. Sometimes, I can move something really light, and it kinda just shakes along in the air. Pretty soon, my concentration snaps, and it ends up shooting against the wall or the floor.

It's funny I think, sometimes. I spend so much time in this house. It's like a whole world's opening up around me, like I've got my own little world in here.

And then there's this world outside, and it's like Mark has his own world, too. He goes off painting and then he stocks shelves at the toy store in the mall. He took on that job a few month ago, to help pay for the medical bills. I should get a job, too, now that I'm feeling better a lot of the time. I probably could go back to Macy's. But it's not consistent yet.

It's funny, though, how we each have our own worlds. And sometimes I wonder if they ever touch. It used to seem like there was just one for both of us, but, after all the headaches, and after this, I don't know...It's like we're not even using the same words. When I say that I've had a good day, how would he know what I mean at all?

June 30
I haven't gotten much of a chance to write over the past few days. A few days ago, we drove to Mark's cousin's house for a cookout.

It was weird being around so many people. Since I left work, I haven't really gotten out much. It was weird because I felt like I had this secret glowing inside of me. And I wanted to shout it all out. I was just the girl with the headaches there, and Mark was just the long-suffering husband. You should have seen the way his aunt put her arms around him. "Oh, Marky," she said. Everyone treated me like I was some piece of thin china or something.

I think it was all the nerves, because my head did start to hurt a little. Mark must have seen me close my eyes, because soon people started to ask me how I was. That didn't help.

I left everyone behind on the deck and went into the kitchen. I tried to focus my mind. Turning my back to the partly covered windows, I picked up a toothpick

and held out my hand. I tried to lift it a little. I
couldn't. I tried again. Then it went up and it stayed
there. I let my mind just hang around it, just trace it
all over. I find that kinda soothing sometimes. It was so
tiny, so very thin.

The slider by the back deck opened, and the toothpick dropped to the ground. It was Mark. I bent down
to pick it up. "Hey," he said.

"Hey."

"You feeling alright?"

I pulled my hand through my hair. I was feeling a
little better. "Yeah. Better."

He leaned back against the table and crossed his
arms. It seemed like he was staring at me through
some pane of bulletproof glass. "So, you having a good
time?"

"It's okay." I started smiling, and he did, too.

"If I have to eat any more of that potato salad, I
think I'll blow." We both laughed. It was like we used to
be, for a minute. We hadn't been that way in so long.

Later, we were driving back. It was dark and starting
to rain a little bit.

Mark seemed to be thinking about something. He
can get like that now—like he's swirling down his own
private whirlpool. Maybe I can be like that, too. I
looked at him. The light of the cars around us and the
headlights and the lights above mixed with the shadows, kinda like a woven basket, kinda like a cage,
around him.

"Mark," I said.

It seemed like a long wait before he spoke, as the
wheels of the car turned over again and again. "Yeah,
Alyssa?" It was like he had to stretch for his voice to
carry.

"You know, I really have been feeling better recently—I mean, about the headaches."

"Yeah," he said, "yeah, you look...different."

I don't know if he really even believed me there.

"Mark." I took a breath. "Have you ever wondered what it would be like to be able to do magic?"

"What—like pull a rabbit out of a hat? Like that book you like—*The Other Side*?" Had something turned in his tone?

"Like—like...whatever."

"I don't know."

His voice seemed almost to be slipping into the shadows. I rushed on and said something, and maybe I shouldn't have. I almost felt like I was about to laugh. "No, really, what would you think?"

"Maybe I'd think I was crazy," he said. It seemed like his eyes were really heavy on me there.

I didn't say anything, then, or for the rest of the whole ride home.

July 8

Today was a record: for the first time in months, I haven't had a headache in a we——

Sorry about that long line. Just as I was writing, I heard a loud smash. Don't worry. It wasn't anything serious; Mark only knocked a glass off the table. Shards were everywhere. He helped me sweep it up. His face was all red. I told him it could happen to anybody. "Yeah, yeah," he kept saying and nodding his head. Men can be funny like that. Like he almost couldn't believe it could happen to *him!*

In any case, I haven't had a headache in a week. That

feels almost like a reason to celebrate. A year ago, I wouldn't have thought that. It shows how things can change.

July 12
I've found a new object to be experimenting with: a brass candlestick Mark and I got as a wedding present (someone gave us two—a matched pair). I've been working with this one. It's nice because it's heavier, but not too heavy, so I can work on trying to move things around. You know how I said that learning to work with this power is like learning to ride a bike? Well, it takes a while to get off the training wheels. I remember, back when I was first trying this power, I couldn't have lifted (not willingly, anyway) anything like this. I tried, once, weeks ago, to lift it. Sweat broke out all over me, but it didn't seem to move a bit.

It's about learning to keep my balance. Sometimes, it's almost easier to keep your balance while moving; sometimes, I can manage a quick *zip* while a slow hovering might be harder. I'm working on moving the candlestick in a circle. I'm getting better at it, I think, even if the circle is more like a square sometimes.

This power's so weird. In a lot of ways, I feel so connected, now, to myself, like I get more how I fit together. I even feel almost more connected to the world, or at least to the things around me.

July 15
It was so hot today. I went outside tonight and watched the fireflies dance. I sat out for a while. The fireflies went somewhere else. The moon was behind a cloud somewhere. The outside light wasn't on. I was just there on the porch. Mark was at work—or somewhere.

He was there in his secret world, and I was in mine. The darkness makes you lonely, sometimes.

July 19
I've been trying to work with multiple objects for the past few days. That's really hard, and it makes my head hurt sometimes. I have to keep all these psychic rings—that's what I'm calling them now, by the way—in place, in two different places. It can be hard to keep things distinct like that. You kinda have to remember how they are relative to each other. You feel the space in between, too. That's what I'm learning more now: to feel the space in between. You might not think it's anything, but I'm learning to feel it—how thick and solid and heavy it can be. I sometimes look at that candlestick spinning in the air and looking out at this vast ocean of space. That space in between isn't nothing. Sometimes I think it's the most solid thing of all.

July 23
Doctor. Doctor. Everything's changed. I've been discovered. I've discovered.

It happened this afternoon. You know that candlestick? Well, I was practicing with it today. I was making it just turn in a circle. I had been having a harder time the past couple days. But I was getting it to work. I was feeling its curves, slipping up the flat base to the lower sections that always reminded me of some fairytale trumpet. Then up the two globes to the opening for the candle. I was so into it that I must not have heard the car pulling into the driveway.
The front door opened. I heard that.

It was Mark. The rings went flying everywhere, and the candlestick dropped to the floor. *Thud.*

How much did he see? Thoughts raced through my head. *What, what, what—*

But Mark looked all calm. He just stood there in the open doorway. His mouth was hovering open in some kind of smile. I saw him breathing, there, his chest rising and falling with slow, stretching breaths.

He didn't look angry or hurt or mad or shocked or freaked out. He just stood there. Then he spoke.

"So you can do that, too?"

The other candlestick left the shelf where it had been and drifted in the air. It floated there, quivering a little, like my husband's chest, but steady still.

It wasn't me. It wasn't just me.

We both smiled as the other one rose to meet its mate.

E. THOMAS FINAN is a native of Massachusetts. He holds degrees from Cape Cod Community College and Boston University. He has taught at Boston University, the University of Massachusetts Dartmouth, and the University of Miami.